I0822852

TURNAROUND

TURNAROUND

Harbert Alexander

Illustrations by Wanda Stanfill

Library of Congress Cataloging-in-Publication Data

ISBN: 979-8-9850605-7-7

Printed and bound in the United States of America by Ingram Lightning Source

First edition

Cover design and illustrations: Wanda Stanfill

Editing, layout, and design: Jacque Hillman, Katie Gould, Kim Thomas Stewart, and Jason Tippitt

Eye injury graphic: Designed by Gregg Bender; information at right given to Harbert Alexander by Dr. Bruce Herron

The HillHelen Group LLC
hillhelengroup@gmail.com

October was the best of times, with the World Series in full swing and baseball at its best. It was the gentle time of year. Spring had arrived early, and summer stayed late.

The season would end all too soon, however. And with it, the game.

The thought always made Cole Adams nostalgic, and particularly so this year.

Outside his window, he watched a group of kids playing baseball near the church next door. The pitcher didn't have a glove. One of the kids, maybe more than one of them, might make it to the majors someday. Probably not. He ought to know.

Cole was one of those dreamers, one who had been part of the big game and now had stepped away. Time to grow up. Time to move on, but he felt out of step. Like a soldier in a parade, he knew the cadence and rhythm, but his footsteps went the wrong way.

Now he had a choice in front of him, and he prayed he'd made the right one. It was a choice that little boys everywhere dreamed of and prayed for.

How comfortable it had been to be a boy, to grow and let go so slowly, to let time ease that transition from growing to grownup. At thirty-two, he had thought he was long past childish dreams. Then his dream came calling. Did he dare give up the comfort of this life he'd built to chase it? Did he even want to?

In his bedroom were two uniforms. Which should he wear, come spring?

Walking to the closet, Cole pushed aside both outfits—one black, one pinstriped—and took out a box. Inside was a weathered baseball glove, the first one he'd bought with his own money. Thinking of the young pitcher next door, he slipped on some shoes and headed for the church, glove in hand.

This baseball dream of his—how had it all begun?

Perhaps, it had begun with a curveball.

God had thrown Cole the first of many curveballs at the age of twelve. He'd been doing his best to catch them ever since.

The children greeted him with wide smiles and cries of excitement.

"Preacher!" shouted Pete, the empty-handed pitcher. "Come and throw a few!"

"Not today," Cole said, tossing Pete the glove. "Today, I'm batting."

***

Young Cole Adams was all legs and arms with not much in between. Klutzy by nature, he would stumble and fall even if there was nothing to fall over.

He was awkward, but friendly and outgoing nonetheless. Perhaps that was because he was a "PK"—a preacher's kid. Not only was his father a preacher, but his two older brothers were also preachers, and his sister was a church secretary.

With an easy smile, brown hair, and blue eyes, Cole wasn't much different from other boys. He only felt like it. And yet, in the summer of his twelfth year, his dreams were within reach.

It was 1987, and his whole world revolved around baseball and the Atlanta Braves. He watched them on television and listened to them on his radio. Though he was only an average student, especially in math, he knew every player's batting average. The walls of his room told the story, with pictures and pennants covering every inch.

And now there was going to be a new baseball league near where he lived in the suburbs of Memphis, Tennessee. He would have his own uniform. He would be a star. An article in the paper said there would be four teams: the Lions, Rotary, Doctors, and Exchange. A new field was under construction with a pitcher's mound, a dugout, and an outfield fence. It should be finished just in time for the season to begin, and tryouts were scheduled.

On reporting day, all of the boys lined up by age and alphabet. Since he was Cole Edward Franklin Adams, he was at the front of the line. When asked for his name, he responded with all four. The coach, after some hesitation, asked, "Which one of those is your first name?"

Before he could answer, a voice at the back of the line said, "Most people call him 'Wormy'!"

There could be little doubt that the remark came from Robert Sullivan, the class bully and clown. He was the one who had saddled Cole with "Wormy"—a jab at Cole's lean, lanky frame. Despite what he'd said, Robert was also the only one who used the dreaded nickname.

Cole ignored him and began filling out the registration forms. Sullivan started up again. "Oh, Wormy! Can that be you? Surely not! Trying out for a baseball team? What's that under your arm? Is that your mommy's purse—full of lipstick and powder? No way that could be a baseball glove!"

Aware that the signup was turning into a shouting contest, the coach split the group. Some boys went out to the field, and the other boys formed a line behind home plate to bat. When it was Cole's turn, he realized that his loudmouthed adversary was going to pitch to him. It was Cole's chance to get even, to shut Sullivan's big mouth. And what's more, if Cole did well, he would have a good chance of making the team.

"Get ready, girly boy, I'm going to put this pitch into your ear!" Sullivan said.

As Cole stepped into the batter's box, he replied, "Hey, Sully, I heard you like geography and history so much, you're going to take them again next year. We're going to miss you in the next grade."

Sullivan's response was a fastball aimed at Cole's head, missing him by inches. The next pitch came in high and tight, hitting Cole just above the elbow. The coach stepped in.

"That's enough for you, Sullivan! Get your butt into the outfield," he yelled.

Not sure that he could swing a bat after being hit, Cole stepped back into the batter's box as a new pitcher stepped onto the mound. Three more pitches ended the misery.

In his dreams, he had hit home runs after home runs. But today he had failed miserably by striking out. One of the coaches told him, "It's all right, kid, you'll get another chance. Go shag flies in the outfield for a while."

As the tryouts continued, it appeared his chance might be over. Desperate for another opportunity, Cole watched in the outfield until a ball came his way. Anxious to show his ability, he took three steps and threw the ball back toward the pitcher's mound. In a moment he would never forget, he watched as the pitcher turned away from him and back toward the batter just as the ball struck him behind the left ear, knocking him to the ground.

As the pitcher struggled to get to his feet and turned to see who had hit him, Cole recognized Sullivan. Knowing he was in real trouble, Cole began walking away in hopes that Sullivan would not recognize him.

As he reached the edge of the field, Sullivan screamed, "Wormy, you're dead meat for that little trick!"

Knowing his only hope was to start running, Cole took off for home. Two blocks from the field, Sullivan caught up and knocked him down with a shoulder block and a kick in the side, followed by a cuff to the face. Scrambling to his feet, Cole took off running again. This time he barely made it around the next corner before being knocked down again. He landed, hard, on his right arm. Pain jolted through his entire side. Sullivan delivered another blow, then took off as a car rounded the corner. The car pulled up and stopped, and a quiet voice inquired, "Cole, are you all right?"

"Yes, Dad. I fell, and my friend was helping me get up."

"Well, let's go home. It's nearly time for dinner."

Cole brushed himself off as his dad said, "Even baseball stars have to eat."

With torn pants, scrapes on his knees and elbows, and red marks on his face, Cole had obviously been on the losing end of a fight.

"Well, how did it go out there? Did you get to bat yet?"

"Oh, yeah," the boy mumbled. "First I got to bat, then I struck out, and, well . . ." Cole began to cry.

Putting his arm around Cole, his father replied, "Who knows, you might be in for a surprise. Remember, I'm a preacher, and I see miracles every day."

"What's for supper?" was Cole's only response.

Two days later, Cole joined a large group of boys to see who had been chosen and what teams they were on. The list was in alphabetical order, with each team listed separately. Cole's heart leapt when he saw the name Adams on the list for the Exchange team, but elation turned to disappointment when he realized it was Chris Adams and not Cole Adams. His name was not on the list. As he turned to leave, a blow hit him in the back and almost knocked him down.

"Don't worry, Wormy, you can be on our team. All of your best friends are there, and you can be our water boy. Hang around a little while so I can finish up what we started two days ago," Robert Sullivan sneered.

Miserable and embarrassed, Cole left the field, going home a different way from before.

It was early May. School would not start again for three months, but for Cole Edward Franklin Adams, summer was all but over.

Cole trudged into his front yard that day with his head down. Meeting him on the porch, Luther Trotter put a hand on his shoulder. A middle-aged black man who worked for the railroad, Luther did odd jobs for the church in the afternoons. He had become a good friend of Pastor Dan's.

"Hey, Cole, your daddy told me he was a mighty fine preacher but not much of a teacher. Said he didn't know much about baseball and for me to see if I could help. Do you reckon I could show you a thing or two?"

Somewhat startled, Cole muttered, "Thank you, Luther, but it's too late for that. Besides, I never knew you knew anything about baseball."

"Might be 'cause you never asked me. Go get me a baseball and bring it back here. Do it quick before your mother finds something else for you to do."

When Cole got back, he saw a log standing up with a soda can on top. "Pretend that's a batter and knock that can off," Luther said.

After three tries, none of which got close to the can, Cole handed the ball to Luther, mumbling, "It's not so damn easy. You think you can do better?"

Luther picked up the ball and with an easy motion threw it toward the can, which exploded off the top of the log. Again, Cole muttered, "Damn."

Luther said, "That word you're using, 'damn,' not such a good word. Try 'durn,' 'dang,' or something like that. Your mother hears you saying 'damn' all the time, you're going to be in lockup for a month or so. Tomorrow you be in my back yard at five o'clock. Your daddy knows you're going to be there. Maybe I can teach you something about throwing a baseball. And don't bring that glove with you—throw that thing away."

By midafternoon the following day, Cole had a list of twenty or more excuses why he was giving up baseball. He had failed in his effort to make a team, gotten hurt and beat up, and been embarrassed in front of his friends. No, sir! He had had enough of that! He busied himself in the yard, staying out of sight, until his father came looking for him at about five fifteen.

"Aren't you supposed to be somewhere at five o'clock? I thought you would be at Luther's house by now."

"I changed my mind," Cole mumbled.

"Well, that's not the plan. You should have talked to me about it. Now, get in the car."

For the second time in a week, Cole had a feeling he had just lost another fight.

Luther, working in his front yard, lifted his hand in a quick wave to Pastor Dan. "Thirty minutes late. Gonna cost you, Cole. Yes, sir, gonna have to work twice as long today—got lots to do, but first, let's go in the house. Pearly Mae is expecting you. You, too, Reverend, you come on."

Unsure, Cole held back until his father nudged him, saying, "Let's go."

The house was small but tidy, with three young boys watching cartoons. An enticing smell lured Cole toward the kitchen.

"See what you almost missed," his father whispered.

Just then Luther's wife, Pearly Mae, emerged from the kitchen. Short, neat, and with a big smile on her face, she helped Cole relax.

"Reverend, so good to see you! I've been thinking about dropping in on your church one day. I heard some folks say you Presbyterians are frozen, or is it chosen?" she teased. "Bet if I brought our choir over there, it would loosen things up!"

"Well, you come on over, Pearly Mae. I suspect we could use some loosening up."

"Y'all come on in the kitchen," Luther said. "Let's see what Pearly Mae has for us. But first, let me introduce you to the children: Socrates is the oldest, then Edison, then Douglas. Their sister, Eleanor, is asleep right now."

"What's it going to be? Apple or cherry pie? And do you want ice cream on it?" Pearly Mae asked. "Reverend, I plan on fattening this boy up, but I have enough for you, too. Which one do you two want—or some of both?"

The pies just out of the oven looked as good as they smelled. Much to his father's amusement, Cole responded, "Apple is my favorite, but I love cherry, too. Could I have a piece of both with a little ice cream?"

"Now, Reverend, how about you? A little pie won't hurt you, and maybe it'll help your voice so you could sing like the Baptists do."

"Pearly, my singing is beyond repair, but I would truly love to have a piece of cherry pie. Just a little slice and a little ice cream, too."

A few minutes later, Luther laughed and said, "Break time is over. We need to get to work. Let's go out to the back yard. Reverend, you come, too, if you have time."

"Thanks, Luther, but I'm better at writing sermons than throwing a baseball. You two have at it."

Once they were outside, Luther handed Cole a glove. "You use this until we get a new one." The glove was old, worn, and had caught a lot of baseballs.

How did he know I was right-handed? Cole wondered silently.

"Welcome to Yankee Stadium; we're going to make you a star. Come on over to the pitcher's mound, and we can get started."

In the middle of the yard was a small pile of dirt—obviously a pitcher's mound. On a fence some distance away was a small, white circle the size of a baseball. Just above it was a dinner bell suspended from an iron triangle. Near the mound was an old canvas bag full of baseballs. "Now you start ringing that bell. When you use all of them balls, go pick them up and start all over.

"Do that two times, and when you're through, I want you to do pull-ups on that bar over there."

Finding it was pointless to resist, Cole picked up a ball and stepped onto the mound. The small, white circle seemed miles away, farther than he could throw.

Noting his hesitation, Luther laughed and said, "Seems like a long way, don't it?"

"About ninety feet or so, I guess," Cole mumbled.

"Well, actually, it's forty-six feet. Exactly what the Little League rules specify and the distance you were when you struck out the other day. And when you grow up and get to the big leagues, you will find it's sixty feet and six inches, but we can wait a few years for that."

Cole threw the ball as far as he could, but it landed short of the plate.

"Come on, Cole, you throw like an old woman. You okay?"

Feeling it was time to tell the truth, Cole admitted, "I got in a fight the other day. My dad doesn't know it, but Robert Sullivan beat me up pretty good. I landed on the sidewalk on my side, and my arm really doesn't feel like throwing a baseball."

"Little friend, it might surprise you that your dad and I both know about that fight. And what we're going to do is learn how to throw a baseball and how to take care of bullies like Robert Sullivan, but that is going to take a little while. The first step is to get you feeling better. Let's go inside and see if Pearly Mae can help. Seems like she's better than old Dr. Skinner and a lot cheaper, too."

Pearly Mae was standing by the door when they came in and asked her to take a look at Cole's injury. "Little man, you take that shirt off—I can't fix what I can't see."

Somewhat embarrassed, Cole pulled off his shirt to reveal an ugly bruise on his side and a right arm with alternating shades of black and purple.

"Oomph, oomph! You must have broken the sidewalk with that one," Pearly Mae said. "Don't see how you lifted a fork to eat the pie, much less throw a baseball. Luther, bring me that special ointment I always use."

As Pearly began to spread a thick, brown cream on the bruises, Cole suddenly came to life.

"Oh, oh!" he gasped. "What is that horrible, horrible . . . it smells like a dead skunk!"

"The worse the smell, the quicker the cure," Pearly Mae replied as she continued to spread more of the offensive cream.

After she finished, Luther said, "Come on, Cole, I'll give you a ride home. It's nearly suppertime. We can worry about baseball tomorrow."

To Cole's surprise, his brothers, Bill and Joseph, and his sister, Cecile, had little to say about the peculiar smell, though he suspected his mother, Rachel, had told them not to mention it.

For the next two weeks, the routine never varied. Luther would pick Cole up, and they would go to Luther's house. As the days passed, the bruises on Cole's side and arm slowly faded, as did the soreness, but his arm didn't have quite the same swing it used to have. Each afternoon, Pearly Mae would have something wonderful ready for them—usually cake or pie. If the pie was apple or cherry, two scoops of ice cream went on the top.

The desserts were the best part of the afternoon, but the rest was another matter. Though Cole tried again and again, it was obvious something was not right. The ball reached the small, white circle once or twice, but usually it bounced on the ground two or three times before it got there. One day, discouraged and embarrassed, he decided to escape. It was much too painful to say goodbye, so he slipped out the side gate to walk home. After no more than a few steps, to his dismay, he saw Luther standing by the gate.

"Going home early, little friend? Pearly would be mighty disappointed if you're gone. She picked up a lot of fresh berries this morning, and a cobbler just came out of the stove. She plans to put some weight on you. Come on in, and you can tell her goodbye."

Realizing it was wrong to resist their kindness, Cole shuffled into the kitchen and was greeted with the smell of a freshly baked dessert.

"I know this is your favorite, Cole, and guessed you was about to say goodbye. I made this for you. Gonna miss having you hanging around."

At a loss for words, Cole could only mutter, "Thank you, Pearly."

As he continued through a record helping, Luther startled him, saying, "Stop, Cole! What did you just do?"

Cole stammered, "Nothing. I didn't do anything!"

With a smile, Luther said, "I've been studying you and your hand. You do a pretty good job with a fork. You get that cake and pie right in your mouth, no trouble at all, but you do it with your left hand.

"Let me tell you a railroad story: Fellow I worked with named Bubby, hard worker, but as the old expression goes, don't think his elevator runs all the way to the top. He can't seem to figure if you want a train to Memphis, you can't be on the track to Baltimore. Train has to be on the right track. Now, I know you're wondering what this has to do with eating dessert. I think your train might be on the wrong track. How come you eat with your left hand and throw a baseball with your right? Doesn't seem natural. What do you think?"

Cole interrupted him, saying, "What's that smell—something terrible?"

"Well, turnip greens are like a lot of things, they got to smell bad before they get good," Luther said. "Ain't nothing much like a mess of greens and big piece of cornbread."

Thinking if he continued the discussion, he might have to sample the greens, Cole changed the subject. "Hey, Luth, you've been fooling me."

"Not sure what you're talking about, but no, I never fooled you."

"Well, something puzzles me," Cole said. "If you're right-handed, how come your glove is always on your right hand and seems like you're always holding the baseball in your left?"

"Well, well, little man, seems like you've finally opened your eyes and looked around. You've been so wrapped up in your own troubles, you never looked to see what the rest of us were doing," Luther said with a chuckle. "One summer when I was about your age, I had a wreck on my bicycle, broke my arm in two places. Summertime, my arm in a cast, all my friends playing ball, figured it would ruin my summer. But no, it didn't. I learned to bat with one hand and throw with my left. I got so good at it, I never went back to my right—simple as that. But that won't work for you."

"What do you mean it won't work for me?" Cole said angrily. "If it worked for you, it would work for me, too."

"No, it won't. Cole, we're different, you and me. I didn't have nothing else but playing ball. You got so many other things that need your attention, like school and girls."

"Think so?" Cole muttered. "We'll see. We'll just see."

Luther's six-year-old son Socrates pushed his head into the kitchen. "Mama says if y'all don't quit arguin' with each other, the pie's gonna give you a stomachache."

Smiling, Luther put his arm around the little boy.

"Tell you what, Sox, maybe it's time to show Mr. Cole our secret room. Show him what we know about baseball," he said, then turned his attention back to Cole. "Maybe you'll know how this all started—why your daddy thinks I can help you. Otherwise, you might grow up and be a preacher like him."

Following Socrates, they moved to a room near the front of the house. The door to the room was closed. "Secret room," whispered the little boy. "Don't many people get in here."

At first, Cole was unsure what he was seeing. One whole wall was covered with pictures and old newspaper clippings. Another wall had shelves with baseballs, mostly with signatures or writing on them. On the far wall were bats and more balls. A large picture near the door caught his eye. A group of baseball players, bats in hand, seemed ready to play.

"Is that you?" Cole stuttered. "You never told me you used to play. Who are those people?"

"Little friend, it's a long story better told another time. Don't have much to do with throwing a ball. You go home and think 'bout it. Quit if you want. We'll still be friends. Pearly gonna miss you. She thinks it's part of her job to keep you filled up. It's late now. Come back tomorrow if you want to, and I'll tell you about those old pictures."

Curious about what he had seen but still determined to quit, Cole returned the next day at four. When he knocked, Socrates cracked the door. Peeping out, he muttered, "Daddy's not home now. Mama's visiting next door. He didn't know whether you was coming but said it was all right to show you the pictures. Mama gots a chocolate cake in the refrigerator; let's us get a piece 'fore they get back. She don't let me have a piece very often, so let's get some."

While they ate a second piece, Socrates said, "My daddy was famous, but he keeps it a secret. Says he's just a railroad man now. He'll be home pretty quick. He'll be surprised about that cake. It was 'posed to go to choir practice tonight. Mama'll be surprised to find half that cake eaten up. 'Spect I'm gonna tell her you ate it."

"Pearly ain't no fool!" thundered a voice from the back door. "Lucky for you, she's got another cake in the freezer. She's got choir practice tonight, and she don't want to disappoint the ladies. Now, come on, Cole, if you want, I'll show you those pictures."

In the baseball room, Cole flipped through photo albums and skimmed articles while Luther shared his story.

"I didn't have much family growing up," Luther said. "Raised by an aunt and uncle. Poor folks, farmers. I figured I was a burden to them, so first chance I got, I ran away. A minor-league baseball team was in town for an exhibition game, and I joined them. Rode all over the country with them in their old bus. Washed their uniforms, cleaned their shoes, ran errands for them."

He was only fifteen when he started, and he ran errands for the team for two years. At seventeen, he joined the team.

"One day, the manager saw me throw a baseball. Now, I could throw a baseball through a barn door. Our best pitcher had a sore arm, and we were going to play an exhibition game in some little town. So they gave me a uniform and said, 'Go pitch.' They thought it'd be funny. Turned out it wasn't so funny. Nobody could hit me. Struck most of them out,"

Luther continued. "They were impressed, sent me to a tryout where I was offered a contract, and I became a professional ball player instead of just the batboy. I played eight years. Played with and against some mighty fine players. Sweet memories in that room, but I don't go in there much. Too many ghosts hanging around."

"Why did you quit? Did you get hurt?" Cole asked.

"No, not that. It was just time. It was pretty special. Big crowds, pretty girls, a little money in my pocket, sort of like a dream for a young boy who never had much. I had fallen in love with Pearly, and we had rented a place. We wanted a house full of children. Trouble was, I was playing ball and away from home for weeks at a time. That just wouldn't work, so I went home. Got lucky to find a job with the railroad, been there ever since," Luther said. "Look around all you want. If I don't get supper going, Pearly will be an unhappy lady."

By the time he got home, Cole was still muttering to himself. "This will be simple. A week or two, I'll show him. Going to be easy."

In the back yard, he walked off a spot about the same distance that Luther had marked off. Not having a glove for his right hand, he decided he would start off throwing tennis balls. In a hall closet, he found a sack of old tennis balls that belonged to his brother.

"These will work as well as baseballs until I get a new glove," Cole said to himself. "They'll work fine, and I can throw off the garage where nobody can see me. Should be pretty easy. Luther did it; I can, too."

Feeling a little awkward, Cole looked around to make sure no one was watching. Then he wound up and threw toward a knot on the shed door. Strangely enough, the ball swerved off to the left, bouncing twice and then rolling to a stop halfway to the shed.

Thinking something was wrong with the ball, he threw a second ball with the same result, only worse. Feeling a little sick in his stomach, Cole kept throwing. He threw all the balls in the bag, but only one reached the shed.

"This is crazy," he mumbled. "Throwing left-handed is no easier than right. It might be harder."

The next day, the pitches got worse instead of better. Finally, on the fourth day, one ball reached the shed, though on the third bounce. On the days that followed, Cole stayed with it, but the results were the same, until something unexpected happened. One afternoon, he was so focused on throwing tennis balls that he was startled to hear a voice behind him.

"What are you doing, Cole?" The voice belonged to Stevie Malone, a boy near his age, nicknamed "Britches" because his pants were always falling down.

"Go home, Britches. What are you doing hiding in the bushes? You scared the fire out of me!"

"I've been watching you, trying to see what you was doing. At first, I thought you was pitching baseballs, but it looks more like you was killing ants."

"Go mind your own business, Britches! Go home!"

As Britches headed home, he stopped and said, "Don't worry, Cole, I won't tell anybody what you're doing. My older brother, Sandy, used to do like that, but my dad bought him a new baseball glove. Expect he'll be pitching for the Yankees or the Cardinals pretty soon."

Once Britches was gone, Cole resumed his efforts. One thought remained, however: a glove. A real glove. No wonder he couldn't pitch. He didn't have a glove, either left-handed or right-handed.

A new glove might cost all the money he had saved up from cutting yards, but it would be worth it. With that thought in mind, Cole headed for a local sporting goods store the next afternoon. It was late in the season and the selection was small, and yet there was a glove just like the ones the big-league players had. It was on sale but still cost more than he had saved. But surely with a glove like that, success and fame were bound to follow. He was trying on the glove, talking to the clerk, when a thump at the front display window made them both jump.

Turning around, Cole saw Robert Sullivan had flung himself into the window to get Cole's attention. Sullivan was making weird, mocking faces at him, pointing to the glove and laughing. Then he mouthed,

"Wormy," and began wriggling against the window like a worm as two of his friends laughed and pointed. Cole's face burned. He turned his back to them.

"Friends of yours?" the salesclerk asked.

"No." Cole gritted his teeth.

Eager to sell a baseball glove so late in the season, the salesclerk reduced the price by ten dollars and threw in two new baseballs. Still, Cole did not have enough money.

The next afternoon, Cole walked by the store one last time, hoping for a miracle. To his surprise, the glove was marked down by fifty percent. Afraid that someone would buy it before him, he ran into the store. The salesclerk hustled to the counter to wait on him.

"Been watching for you. I felt like you might be by this way. Want me to wrap it up?"

"No, no, I'll just take it out."

And yet even with the beautiful new glove and two new baseballs, the problem would not go away.

The easiest solution would be to go back to Luther, but Cole's pride would not let him do that. He would save that for later when he could pitch. Counting his remaining money, including the change, he had just over three dollars left. He knew what to do with it. That afternoon, he went behind the garage again, making as much noise as possible. A few minutes later, he noticed movement in the bushes behind him.

"What are you doing, Britches? Spying on me?"

"Nothing, Cole. Just watching."

"Tell you what, Britches, you want to earn some money?"

"Yeah, sure, Cole. How much?"

"Well, I need someone to pitch to. What if I pay you a quarter to catch for me?"

Never hesitating, Britches replied, "Gonna go get my glove. Be back in a minute."

After giving Britches a quarter, Cole began to pitch. Even with the new glove, the results were the same.

Finally, Britches said, "Hey, Cole, you're wearing me out. Let's try something different. Try pitching underhand and let me get a little closer. Try catching the ball in that fancy new glove of yours, then toss it back to me. Each time, take a step back farther."

To Cole's surprise, pitching underhand was much easier. Every afternoon, they pitched until dark, getting a little farther apart each time. By the end of the fourth day, Cole was running out of quarters and ways to pay Britches, and the space behind the garage was growing too small.

That night at supper, Cole was startled when his father said, "Looks like the back yard is getting a little small for you. That old field behind the church used to be a baseball diamond, you know. Hasn't been used in years. I think there's an old pitcher's mound still there. What if I pay you five dollars to cut the grass, and you could practice there without bothering anybody?"

Though Cole wondered how long his father had been watching him, he leapt at the idea, and by the next afternoon, he was busy cutting grass with his old push mower. Mowing places that were knee-high, Cole had cut all the grass by the end of the second day, and he had five dollars—or, to put it another way, enough quarters to keep Britches catching and returning balls for the next three weeks.

Cole could never tell you how it happened, nor could he understand it himself, but one day he no longer threw underhand and instead raised his arm to throw sidearm. It wasn't perfect or good at first. Balls were sailing left and right of Britches but rarely to him. However, Cole got a little better every day, and as he improved, he began to throw harder. One day, Britches held up his hand and said, "No more, Cole, my hand is killing me. You need to find someone else to throw baseballs with."

It was near Thanksgiving, months since Cole had seen Luther. Maybe it was time to see if Pearly was still making cakes and pies. But what if he wasn't welcome?

Cole had left in a huff, after arguing with Luther. Maybe he shouldn't have gone, but after all, he had learned to pitch left-handed. There was only one way to find out. Time to quit worrying about it and go see if Luther would help. He put his glove in a sack along with one other item. Shortly after buying the new glove, he had glued Robert Sullivan's picture to a chunk of wood for target practice. He'd found that picture in his school desk one day and had known the bully put it there for him to find. It was a page from the newspaper, which had printed a photo of each team in the league with all the players' names.

When Cole practiced throwing the ball, he used Robert Sullivan for a target. Maybe Luther would think it was funny, but he would understand. If Robert Sullivan had not embarrassed Cole and bullied him, he wouldn't have been so determined to throw that ball and throw it well. Even so, he didn't plan on thanking the bully the next time they met. With thoughts of how he would destroy Robert, he was startled when a voice behind him said, "Go on in, Pearly's been expecting you. It'd be a shame for that pumpkin pie to go to waste."

Regaining his composure, Cole asked, "How did you know I was coming?"

"Just had a feeling I might see you today," Luther replied. "Go on in. You keep fooling around, and the ice cream is going to melt."

Cole was inspected by Pearly, who declared, "Child, you've about wasted away since I last saw you. You may need to eat two pieces of pie today."

After they finished the pie, Luther led Cole outside to practice.

"Cole, do you have anything to show me? What have you got in that sack?"

"Not much, just some old schoolwork," Cole replied. Taking a ball out, he threw it toward his old target. This time, he threw it with his right hand; after a series of bounces, the ball rolled to a stop well short of the target. "Whatcha thinking, Luther?"

Pausing, he answered carefully, "Well, Cole, good try."

Laughing, Cole pulled the new glove out.

"Well, well, look at you now. Knew you were up to something."

Pulling out the piece of wood with Robert Sullivan's picture on it, Cole stuck it on the fence next to his old target.

"Now what?" Luther asked.

"Just watch!"

The ball struck just above Robert Sullivan's picture with a sound like a rifle shot.

"My, my," Luther mumbled. "I believe you made a hole in the fence. I suspect that would be quite a surprise to those fellows at the Little League park. Tell you what, Cole, baseball season is still months away. You know how to throw a baseball now. Next, I want you to learn how to pitch. Let me watch you for a little while. You warm up, and then we'll see about someone to catch."

Thinking he would be pitching to Luther, Cole continued throwing balls at the picture of Robert Sullivan. In a few moments, Luther reopened the gate, and to Cole's surprise, Britches was with him.

"I thought you might be tired of throwing at the fence," Britches said.

Seeing Britches, Cole began to sense that somehow Luther might have been closer than he thought. His memory turned to the salesclerk who had suddenly dropped the price on his new glove and given him two new baseballs. Seeing Cole's confusion, Luther said, "Don't be worrying about who done what, just throw the ball," and so the pattern was set.

For the next few months, Britches and Cole would arrive after school, eat whatever Pearly offered, and pitch for an hour or so. Even when the weather was bad, rain or snow, they continued their routine. Sometimes Luther's kids would run around, trying to get in the game. The younger kids always gave up quickly and ran off to play tag a safe distance away, but Socrates was always around, fetching balls and copying his dad in barking out orders. The boys took it in good humor, sometimes pretending to listen to their pint-sized "coach" instead of Luther.

One cold afternoon in early February, Luther changed the game. Bringing out a paper plate and a bat, he sent Britches to the end of the yard behind Cole.

"Now, Cole, I'm going to be a hitter, you're the pitcher, and Britches can be the center fielder. This old paper plate is going to be home plate. You can pretend I'm Robert Sullivan—ought to be easy. As hard as you throw, doubt I'll even see the ball."

Not sure what to expect or what the purpose was, Cole lobbed the first pitch toward the plate. For Cole, the sound of the bat and the arc of the ball far over Britches's head was more than he had expected. *If that's the way this game is played, we'll see what he can do with a fastball,* Cole thought.

This time, the result was even worse, with the ball striking the old fence far behind Britches. Four more pitches produced similar results. After the sixth pitch, Luther held up his hand and asked, "Cole, what have we learned today?"

"Not very damn much," he murmured. "Don't have it figured out yet, but I will."

"Let me give you a hint or two. The first pitch you threw was a good one, but then you threw the next five pitches exactly the same. A blind man could hit the third or fourth pitch no matter how hard you threw. Pitching to a batter is like the old game of cat and mouse. He's got to guess what you're going to throw and what speed you throw. At the same time, you've got to throw him what he's not expecting. Let's try it again."

This time was different but not a lot. Luther hit four out of six pitches over the fence, but Cole did get him to swing and miss twice before they decided to take a break.

"While we're talking about hitting, let me bring up a different subject," Luther said. "It's been almost a year since you tried out for Little League. You're not the same little boy you was back then. All those cakes and pies put some weight on you—some muscle, too. You got some reason to think Robert Sullivan is your friend now? Or is he still the same bully he used to be?"

"You should've seen him last week, Luther," interrupted Britches, who had hung around hoping for a piece of cake or pie. "He elbowed his way in front of us in the lunch line. Then he says to Cole, 'Get your old glove and be ready.' Said he had some new tricks to show him."

Changing the conversation, Luther said, "Let's go see if Pearly's got anything to eat. Then we'll come back and try some new tricks of our own."

A fresh buttermilk pie just out of the oven helped to get over bruised feelings. When they returned to the back yard, Luther put his arm around Cole's shoulders, something he had never done before.

"I ain't going to preach to you. Your daddy's a preacher—not me," Luther said. "But think about this. It's been nearly a year since Robert Sullivan embarrassed you, knocked you down on the ground, beat you up. He's most likely going to do it again. Do you think he's changed? Do you expect him to put his arms around you and say he's sorry?"

Luther stood back and patted his shoulder.

"The Bible was pretty specific when it tells you to turn the other cheek, but you do that by being courteous to that boy," he said. "When he crosses a line, what are you gonna do? You're a lot bigger than when we started working. But think about this. If he does like he did before, hurts you, makes you look like a fool, are you going to just waste a year trying to throw a baseball? All these afternoons for nothing? What are you gonna do when he starts it again? Go on home and think it over."

It had been a miserable day. Sometimes Cole moved ahead, but then reality crept in like the old saying, "One step forward, two steps back." Or maybe it was three. In time, he could work out something on fooling hitters. He could learn how to outsmart them. But Robert Sullivan was another matter. The more Cole thought about it, the more certain he was that the problem would not go away.

He was standing in Luther's front yard at four o'clock the next afternoon. As usual, Britches was hanging around, hoping for dessert. It had begun to rain by the time Luther got home. To his surprise, he found two cold, wet boys in his garage. "What are you boys up to? Pearly Mae and the boys are gone to the movie, with not a thing here to eat. I've got some peanut butter and jelly. We could make some sandwiches."

"No, Luther. I've got something else to ask you," Cole said. "Don't have anything to do with food or baseball, either. Seems like I've got a rock in the middle of the road, and there's no way to get where I'm going unless I figure some way to get around it or move it. Best way to solve the problem is to move the rock. You know who the rock is. It's up to me to move it. I never thought I would ask you this, but you need to teach me how to fight."

"Well, little friend, I suspect you're right, but I'm not the person to do that. I've got a friend who owes me a favor. I believe he can show you how to solve the problem, but let's make us a sandwich first. Tomorrow, we'll take us a little trip."

Cole was waiting when Luther got home at four the next afternoon.

"Keys are in the car, and we'll take a ride," Luther said. "I'm gonna take you to a place you've never been before. But first, you got to agree to these rules. You're a whole lot bigger than you were a year ago. Bigger. Stronger. Lots more muscle. Now, one, never start a fight. Two, walk away from a fight if you can. But if a fight can't be avoided, hit the other guy first. Hit him as hard as you can and keep hitting him as long as you can. Don't let him hit you."

A short drive later, they reached an old brick building. Out front was a sign with faded letters, "Big Boys Boxing and Self-Defense." Inside, five or six older men were sitting in a group, laughing and reminiscing. When they spotted Luther, all conversation stopped. Then a chorus of greetings broke out. "Where have you been? We heard you died." Others chimed in with similar comments.

Luther took the good-natured ribbing in stride.

"Gentlemen, I'd like you to meet a special friend of mine," Luther said, patting Cole on the shoulder. "This is Cole Adams, who is a fine, young baseball player. Problem is, a bully seems determined to keep him from playing. Now, we need some help. He don't want to be a boxer. Just needs to know how to take care of himself."

One of the men spoke up. "I expect I could teach him a trick or two. Don't much care for bullies anyway."

"How do you know Luther?" Cole asked the man, whose name was Freddy.

"I expect everybody around here knows Luther. He's pretty famous in these parts. Now let's give them time to tell each other all their same old stories, while I show you how to fight."

When Freddy stood up, the room seemed to get smaller. Cole had never seen anyone that big before and with no sign of fat. Cole could see Luther watching him.

"Hey," Luther said. "Better do what he says."

"No fooling," Cole replied.

Taking a step closer, Freddy said, "Hey, Cole, do you like to dance?"

"Not much," Cole mumbled, looking somewhat alarmed.

"Well, when you box, it's sort of like dancing. Your feet have to keep moving," Freddy said, dropping into a loose stance and showing him some footwork. Cole did his best to copy Freddy's moves. "Can't stay in one place. Move your feet like you're doing. Keep your head up. Watch the dude who's bothering you. You watch his eyes. If you think he's going to hit you, hit him first as hard as you can. Then keep hitting him. Don't let up until he gives up. If he hits you first, most times you're going to lose. Remember, never fight if you don't have to. If you gotta fight—don't lose. Are you right-handed?"

"I used to be, but now I guess I'm both."

"Maybe he don't know that. He might be looking in the wrong place. You can fake hitting him with your right hand and hit him with your left hand, then with the right," Freddy said, demonstrating with a couple of fake swings. "Keep doing that until he's had all he wants. Now, you see that bag over there? I want you to put on those gloves and start punching that bag. Keep those feet moving. Look at that bag and pretend it's him. If you do it right, that will be the end of your problems. Maybe we'll get a buddy to box with you someday, but for now, be here around four every afternoon."

As they were leaving, Luther said, "No need to bother your mother with this. It'll just worry her. Your daddy and I think this might get some things straightened out."

For the next few weeks, Cole trained at the gym. He had his fill of hitting the bag first with a left, then a right. Late one Friday, Freddy stopped him, saying, "Little surprise, Cole. Let's see if you have learned anything. See if you can last two rounds with my friend Jonas. Jonas, you be nice to him, you hear?"

Jonas! He knew Jonas. Thinking it was a joke, Cole climbed into the ring. A moment later, Jonas joined him in the ring. In his late fifties, Jonas was much shorter and thinner than Cole.

"Okay, boys. Go to it. Be easy on each other."

Cole stood there, not sure what to do, when Jonas hit him fast—and then hit him three more times.

"Whoa! Stop! That's enough," Freddy said. "Now how did that happen? Cole, you sat there flat-footed, forgot to put your arms up, and didn't try to hit Jonas before he hit you. Good thing I stopped it. These past few weeks have been a waste of time. Get your street clothes on and go home. When you see that bully you've been worrying about, be ready to run."

"No, no! That's not right," Cole protested. "I'm not running from anyone! Not from you, or Jonas, nor Robert Sullivan, or anyone else! I wasn't ready, but that won't happen again. Get your hands up, Jonas. We'll finish this!"

In later years, Cole often wondered if it had been a setup. Perhaps this was all designed to wake him up. "Get your hands up, Jonas, right now. Round two is beginning."

It should have been easy. Jonas had watched him train. He knew Cole liked to fight with his right hand, then follow with a left. Cole didn't do it that way. Not that time. Cole hit him with a left to the chin, and it was over. It wasn't a knockout, but Jonas's eyes gazed at something far away.

"That's enough, Cole!" Freddy said. "Reckon you've learned a thing or two after all."

Baseball tryouts were coming up fast. Cole felt sure he would be chosen for a team. He was much larger than the year before. He was not only taller but stronger. Hopefully, he would not get beaten up again.

On the day of the tryouts, all the boys gathered around the coaches to be split into groups.

At first, it did not seem that Robert Sullivan was there, but then Cole heard his voice rising above the noise of the crowd. When Sullivan saw Cole, his voice seemed to reach another level. "Hey, look what's crawled up once again! Am I going to have to teach you another lesson? Maybe last year wasn't enough!"

"I didn't come here looking to fight you," Cole said. "I don't want to fight you, but I will if that's what you want. Right now, I plan to play baseball."

"Don't really care what you plan to do. I plan to put a whooping on you. Gonna make you forget about baseball."

Just as Cole put his glove down, one of the coaches ran up. "Okay! All right! Let's see who wants to play baseball! Do we have anybody here who thinks he can pitch?" Three boys, including Cole, volunteered to pitch.

"Okay, let's do it this way, ten of you go out in the field. Outfield or infield, wherever you like," the coach said. "The other ten of you will hit, and then you can swap. Each one of you try pitching to five batters. Let's go. Not much time. Somebody grab a bat. The tallest of you can give me your name and pitch."

Cole was the tallest of the three, so he went first. Before he started, he asked, "Do you want them to hit or can I pitch normal?"

The coach laughed and said, "Go ahead and show me what you got."

With that, Cole struck out the first two batters. The third batter hit a groundball to first base. The fourth batter was a tall first baseman. Cole knew he had played the year before and was one of the best hitters in the group.

From the way the first baseman stepped into the batter's box, it was obvious he expected to hit anything thrown to him. Four pitches later, he was another strikeout victim. Laughing, the batter turned to the coach and said, "When you decide to divide up the teams, I want to be on his team. Thought I could hit whatever he threw, but I can't."

With only one last hitter, it had been a perfect afternoon. The other coaches were watching Cole. It was apparent one of the teams would choose him. He could almost feel his new uniform. What would Luther or his dad say when they saw him? There was only one more batter, and who could it be but Robert Sullivan?

"Come on, pitcher, end of the road," Sullivan said. "Just like last year."

When Sullivan stepped in to hit, Cole imagined the hundreds of times he had thrown at the tin can or shed door. Pretending he was throwing at the can, he threw his best fastball inside, just an inch or two under Sullivan's chin.

Thinking Cole was trying to hit him, Sullivan jumped out of the way. Ball one.

Pitch two was in the same place. Again, Sullivan jumped back as the ball curved perfectly over the plate. Strike one. The third pitch was a slow curveball that Sullivan swung at and missed. Strike two. The last pitch was a hard curve that broke in and down from the batter. Strike three. Game over.

Sullivan threw his bat down and pointed to an area behind the dugout, a space Cole would have to walk through to return home.

When Cole started home, he found a crowd already there anticipating the fight. Sullivan stood in the middle of the group, rubbing his hands together. "Well, well, look who's here. Figured you would try to run."

"I don't want to fight you, Sullivan. I could teach you how to hit a curveball or fight you. Your choice."

"Put him down, Robert! He made you look like a fool!" came from one of Robert's followers.

"You shut your mouth, Edwards, unless you feel like fighting this afternoon!" Britches yelled.

With that distraction, Robert Sullivan decided to fight. As he moved toward Cole, Cole stepped back, put his hands up, and began to shuffle his feet. Cole faked with a right and hit Robert with a left to his face.

Caught off guard, Robert tried to step back. Before he could do so, Cole hit him again.

Robert stepped back and turned to regroup. Then Cole ran at him, hitting him three more times in the face before delivering a right to his stomach, and it was all over. Robert was down and trying to throw up.

The whole encounter had taken seconds, but it had been in the works for over a year—every time Cole had thrown a baseball.

When Cole reached home, it was obvious his parents knew about the fight. His mother was working on supper in the kitchen and kept her back to him. His dad stood up and pointed to the back yard.

Since the fight, Cole had kept his emotions to himself. When he reached the spot where his father was standing, he exploded. "I couldn't help it. It wasn't my fault. I tried not to fight him. He wouldn't let me. You know what he did to me last year. I offered to be his friend. I even helped him to get up when it was over. I'm your son; it's not right for you to be mad at me."

Expecting to be admonished or even given a whipping, Cole received a response that surprised him.

"Whoa now, little man. I'm not mad at you. You did what you had to do. Your mom and I just hope you never have to do it again. And Luther and Pearly Mae sent a whole cherry pie for you. Now go inside, clean up, and let's see what your mom has cooked for dinner."

Years later, Cole would remember every word of the conversation and the warmth of his father's hug as they went in for dinner. At school the next day, everyone wanted to talk about the fight. Even some of the girls seemed to notice him for the first time.

Oddly enough, the fight seemed to deflate the meanness right out of Robert Sullivan. Stomping toward Cole in the hall that morning, bruises smeared across his cheekbone and beneath his eye, the class bully looked like trouble. When the other boy raised his arm, Cole expected a rematch—and got a fist bump instead.

"Adams," his former nemesis said, nodded a greeting, and went on to class.

And that was that. Robert Sullivan never called him Wormy again.

Uncomfortable with all of the attention, Cole tried to concentrate on baseball and which team would choose him as their pitcher. As usual, Britches continued to hang around Cole between classes.

"Bet any team would like to have you," Britches said. "Nobody else pitches like you do. Just wish I could be on the same team as you. My dad wants me to do travel ball, though. That's where he played and he says it'd be real fun for me."

"We'll know by this afternoon. The new team rosters are supposed to be posted in the gym by two."

Morning classes seemed to last forever; even the lunch break seemed to go on for hours. After lunch, Cole had biology class, which lasted until two thirty. When at last class was over, the race was on to the gym. It was impossible to see the list with the boys jumping up and down trying to see their names.

Cole knew he wasn't the same as last year, yet memories of disappointment lingered.

Finally, Cole could see the names on the typed list. Two teams were on the first sheet. The names were not listed alphabetically but by position.

The pitchers were at the bottom of each page. Cole's name was not on either of the teams.

The other two teams were on the second page. Knowing his name would be on one of them, Cole scanned quickly. Once again, his name was not listed.

Thinking his name might be listed for some other position, Cole went through the team rosters again—his name was not there. He had been overlooked.

Red-faced, angry, and upset, Cole turned and began walking away before he heard his name called. It was Mr. Stanton, the chemistry teacher.

"Come upstairs to my office, and let's have a talk," Stanton said.

Though he was in no mood to talk to anyone about anything, Cole was afraid not to see what the teacher wanted. When they reached Stanton's office, he wasted no time with small talk.

"I've been waiting for you to come see the list," Stanton said. "Were you surprised your name was not on the list? Do you want to know why you were left off? It doesn't have anything to do with baseball. I watched you yesterday. You were much better than any of the other pitchers. No one else was even close."

"Then why am I not on the list?"

"Pure and simple. You broke the rules," Stanton said. "Not really your fault, but fighting on school grounds is against the rules. I know all about Robert Sullivan. I know he bullied you. I know about last year. The whole thing is wrong, but perhaps there is another way. What would you think about trying out for a spot on one of the travel-ball teams? The players are a little older than you and more experienced. One of the teams has a coach who is a good friend of mine, and he would be glad to let you try out."

"Thanks, Mr. Stanton, but I doubt if my dad would let me play travel ball. They play on weekends, and he won't like that, being a preacher."

"Well, Cole, I certainly understand where you're coming from. If anything changes in the next day or so, let me know."

Knowing there was no chance, Cole headed home. Thinking he

might avoid a confrontation with his father, at least for a little while, Cole slipped into the house through the kitchen, where his sister was waiting for him.

"You do something wrong? Dad is waiting for you in his office."

"No! No, I didn't do anything wrong. I've just had a bad afternoon, and I don't want to talk about it."

Knowing it was useless to avoid his father, Cole trudged up the stairs. His father's office, where he composed his sermons, was at the end of the hall. He kept his office door shut so he might smoke a cigar without Cole's mother complaining about the odor. Cole could not remember a single time his brothers or sister had ever entered.

When Cole knocked on the door, his dad said, "Come in, come in. You want a cigar?"

"No, no, thank you."

"Well, have a seat. How was your day?"

"Trouble. Not good at all."

"So I heard. So I heard. I know all about the school situation—very unfortunate, nothing we can do about it. How bad do you want to play baseball?"

"I really wanted to play. I worked hard to be a good player, but things just didn't work out."

"Yes, you did. Your mom and I were very proud of you. I might have a way you could play."

"But, Dad, the travel-ball teams play on Sundays, and I would have to miss church."

"There are lots of ways to serve the Lord besides sitting in a church pew on a Sunday morning, and I've got something in mind for you. Do you know Mrs. Wilson?"

"Well, I think I do."

"A woman with three children, sits in the back of the church."

"Yes. Pretty sure I know who you're talking about, but what's that got to do with me playing baseball?"

"Here's what I'm willing to do. You work for her three afternoons a week, and you can play ball."

"What sort of work?"

"They heat their house with a wood-burning stove. You can split wood and bring the wood in, help plant a garden, look after the three-year-old, play with the two older children. Oh, and something I forgot, the church is willing to give them twenty-five dollars a week to help them out with groceries. I would expect you to take them the money and do some shopping for them. Before you agree, let's go take a look."

Fifteen minutes later, they were on the edge of town. The Wilsons' home was a small-framed building with little paint. Even though the weather was warm, there was a brick chimney with smoke coming out of it.

"Seems warm for a fire, doesn't it?" was Cole's first impression.

"No, son, I expect she's cooking supper. I know she doesn't have an oven—uses her wood-burning stove. First thing you would need to do is cut the grass. You could use the same mower you use to cut the grass behind the church. When you get the lawn done, we might see if Luther knows anybody with a small tractor who could come and break up enough ground for a garden."

As they were talking, Mrs. Wilson appeared at the door. A small child was holding her hand tightly.

"Please come in, Reverend, and thank you for coming. This little one is my daughter, Christine. Her brother and sister call her Chrissy. The twins, James and Sarah, are eight."

"Well, Mrs. Wilson, this is my son, Cole. He is a baseball player. The problem is that his team plays travel ball and goes all over this part of West Tennessee and North Mississippi. He will be playing baseball on weekends throughout the summer, which means he would miss church. I have agreed to that if he works for you three days a week. He can keep your yard cut, split wood for your stove, and get a garden going. You remember that the ladies' auxiliary at the church is going to help out with a check for twenty-five dollars a week until you get on your feet. Cole can do the shopping for you. Does this sound agreeable for you?"

"Yes," Mrs. Wilson replied in a low voice, and Cole realized she was crying. "It's been hard ever since Ed got sick, and we've just been overwhelmed since he died six months ago. Thanks to you and your son, we'll get back on our feet."

"I know you will. What do you think, Cole?"

"I'll be here tomorrow with a lawn mower," Cole replied.

Later he asked his dad, "What happened to her husband?"

"Some sort of lung cancer. Been sick for several years. Are you good with this arrangement? Do we have a deal?"

"Yes, sir. When we get home, I'll go see Mr. Stanton, see if he still has a place for me."

It was the next day before Cole could make contact with Mr. Stanton. He was delighted that Cole could try out to join the travel-ball team and introduced him to the coach.

"I have no concern about your ability to pitch," the coach said. "I suspect you are throwing better than any pitcher we will face; however, you have no game experience. You have not batted or fielded your position. These are things we will work on. When we are here, we will play our games at City Field adjacent to the Little League field. Saturday mornings, we will practice there and play a game in the afternoon. On Sundays, we usually travel and play two games wherever we go. Be there at nine in the morning. I will have a uniform waiting for you. Any questions?"

"How many games do you play?"

"Well, we are scheduled to play sixty games."

"Wow. That's more than twice what the Little League plays. See you Saturday!"

The next afternoon, Cole talked his dad into helping him carry the lawn mower to Mrs. Wilson's house. The yard hadn't been cut in at least a year. The grass and weeds were up to Cole's knees and had to be cut two or three times. Soon after he started, James and Sarah came out to watch. As Cole struggled with the weeds, he became aware that the eight-year-old twins were following him.

"Hey, Cole, you better watch out," James shouted.

Stopping his mower, Cole responded, "Watch out for what?"

"Snakes! Big snakes!"

"Where?"

"Right over there, can't you see the grass moving?"

Cole jumped back in alarm. Grabbing a shovel, he poked the grass where the snake was hiding. When he did so, a rabbit jumped out.

"I thought you said it was a snake!"

"Well, I thought it was!" James said. "We've been watching the grass move. I knew something was in there. I guess he was waiting for you to get the garden fixed so he can have something to eat."

"Going to be looking down the wrong end of a shotgun if he does," Cole said under his breath.

A few minutes later, James stopped him again. "Cole, can I ask you something? When you get all this grass cut, will you teach us how to play baseball?"

"Well, let me finish this and see about a garden, and then we can play baseball."

Late that afternoon, Cole dropped in on Luther.

"Well, well, it's Farmer Adams come to town."

"I guess you've been talking to my father," Cole replied.

"Seems like I did hear something about you cutting grass and raising a garden."

"Yes, as I expect you know, that's what I'm doing to be allowed to miss church and play travel ball this summer. Part of my work for Mrs. Wilson has me helping with the kids and keeping the grass cut and raising a garden. That ground is hard as a rock; no way I can bust it up. Do you know anyone who has a small tractor? I could pay them to do it, and when that's done, someone needs to show me how to raise a garden."

"Well," Luther said. "I expect I know someone who could break the ground up, normally charge twenty dollars. Expect we could get it done for about half that. We can worry about what seeds and plants you need after the ground is right. All this talk about food is making me hungry. Let's go inside and see what Pearly's been cooking."

Later, after cherry pie and ice cream, Luther asked Cole how his baseball practice was coming.

"Sort of like gardening, it's a learning process," Cole said. "You taught me how to pitch, and I guess I taught myself how to throw a fastball, but until now I never played an inning of baseball. Lots to learn, but it's what I wanted to do."

Three days later, Luther's friend Ernest showed up with a tractor that looked like a junkyard relic but ran like a top and soon turned Mrs. Wilson's back yard into something that looked like the cover of a gardening magazine. The job cost ten dollars but was well worth it. Next, Luther put Cole in the front seat of his truck and the twins climbed into the back for a trip to the hardware store. The final purchase was for a ball of twine, a dozen tomato stakes, and thirty wooden stakes. On the way back to the garden site, Luther seemed to get lost and they ended up at Luther's house, where Pearly introduced them to apple pie and ice cream. She sent a whole pie in a box for Mrs. Wilson.

The next afternoon, Luther had Cole place a stake in the ground, then another stake three feet away from it, and then another until all fifteen stakes were in a straight line. They went to the other end of the garden and repeated the procedure. A piece of string was then stretched from one peg to the peg at the other end of the garden. When they were finished, they had fifteen lines stretched across the garden. Using a hoe, they followed the string and made trenches, and then Cole put seeds and plants in the trenches, as Luther came behind him and covered up the seeds. Twelve tomato plants were placed on the outside of the fifteen lines in the dirt.

James was quick to point toward a patch of grass near the end of the yard. "Looky there! He's been watching us all afternoon. Don't you see those big eyes?"

"Well, it's just a rabbit," Luther said. "James, we'll make a trap and you can keep him for a pet. If you feed him kitchen scraps, it will keep him from eating up the garden. What are you going to name him?"

"Well, I already got his name picked out."

Luther said, "I'll bet it's Peter Rabbit."

"No, his name is Snake."

"I've never heard of a rabbit named Snake."

"Well, the first time we saw him, we thought he was a snake." So the name the little boy chose for his rabbit became permanent. Luther produced an old wooden trap with a carrot as the bait. It only took a day for Snake to give up his freedom. By the end of the week, the box trap was no longer needed as Snake followed James wherever he went.

The vegetables were slow to get started; not so with the grass and the weeds that needed constant attention. When Cole wasn't working in the garden, he split wood or helped with the children.

Raising a garden and taking care of the children were learning experiences, but so was being part of a baseball team. Even though Cole could throw a baseball faster than almost anyone, he had never batted or fielded a groundball. At least his buddy Britches was right there with him. He'd landed a spot on the same team as Cole. Both boys had a lot to learn.

Though they were members of the Shelby Tigers baseball team, they played very little for the first part of the season. Unless something happened, Cole figured they would warm the bench for the year. He listened to his coach, who put it clearly: "Cole, you throw harder than almost anybody in the league, but they have more experience. Most players on the team were with us last year. For some, it will be their third year. Stay with us for a few years, and we'll get you a real good scholarship to play ball in college. Don't get in a hurry; we play a lot of games."

For the first ten games, Cole sat on the bench, getting in only one game as a pinch-hitter. When he finally got to pitch, he did not do very well. The coach went over his performance, pitch by pitch.

As Cole learned to watch the batters and listen to his coach, he improved. By the end of the season, he had learned a lot, and he had grown close to a number of his teammates, especially Sparky Andrews, his catcher, and Don and David Nixon, twin outfielders. They were the best hitters on the team.

It was a long, hot summer. Cole had never raised a garden, and he had to watch three-year-old Christine, who wanted to help him by pulling up the tomato plants. James and Sarah delighted in taking Snake around the neighborhood in a wheelbarrow.

One day while Cole was cutting and splitting wood, Mrs. Wilson called him into the kitchen. "Here, try this," she said as she handed him a warm piece of cornbread. The treat of the cornbread became a daily event, much in the way Pearly's pies had been.

Everything seemed to grow in the warm summer days. Luther came by every week to check on the garden, make sure the grass and weeds were under control, and see that the cornbread was to his liking.

"You know," Luther said. "Everything is growing pretty good—even you. How much have you grown? Seems like a lot."

"Not sure, but I got a lot of clothes that don't fit me anymore," Cole said.

"Even that rabbit has grown. We ought to get a skillet and some hot grease and have some fried rabbit." These remarks produced hails of protest from everyone, including little Christine. "Just kidding, I promise. I promise to leave Snake alone, but I might take more of those greens home for Pearly."

Every week, Cole and Britches took batting practice in the field behind the church. Luther knew someone who had pitched for years for a team from Luther's church. The boys agreed to pay him ten dollars a week.

Gradually, they began to improve. They didn't play in every game, but more and more, they became an integral part of the team.

Luther watched and coached the two boys on what they did right and what they did wrong. It was a new experience for one who had always been a pitcher, rather than a batter. Both boys swung and missed ninety percent of the pitches. Luther showed them no mercy. When they swung and missed, Luther called, "Timeout! Where are your eyes? Where are your hands? He is throwing the same pitch at the same speed every time. Can you not see that? Pearly is not handing out any more pieces of pie or cake if y'all don't wake up!"

Both boys were natural athletes, and by the third week, Cole and Britches were much improved. Over cake and ice cream the last afternoon, Luther said, "You watch, nearly all the pitchers that you play against have one pitch and one speed. Watch and be ready."

Cole's chance came two weeks later, not to pitch but to play right field when the regular player twisted his ankle and couldn't play. It was the seventh and last inning when Cole came to bat. There were two runners on base but already two outs. Behind him, Cole could hear his teammates saying, "Looks like this one's over. Afraid we've lost again."

The first two pitches had been curveballs; Cole guessed the pitcher would throw a fastball to end the game. It didn't end the way they expected. At first, it looked like Cole had hit a high fly ball toward center field, and then they realized the center fielder had stopped and was looking up and behind him.

"Home run! Home run! I've never seen a ball go that far. They'll never find that ball."

There would be other home runs. There would be other wins, but never another one like that. Cole's teammates hoisted him on their shoulders and carried him to the bus, chanting, "Adams, Adams!" It was a night he would not soon forget.

By midsummer, the garden seemed to explode. Tomatoes, corn, peas, squash, and okra filled the kitchen, with Mrs. Wilson cooking and canning food for the winter. The best part of the hot summer afternoons was when Luther would stop by and they would cut up a watermelon. Even Mrs. Wilson and little Christine joined in.

One afternoon, Cole was splitting wood when he heard voices in the garden. Turning around, he saw two boys about his age pulling tomatoes off the vine and dropping them in a basket.

"Hey! What are you doing?"

"Well, glad you asked. We wanted some of your garden stuff to sell at the farmer's market down the road."

"Who gets the money?" Cole asked.

"Not you, stupid! We take what we want, kind of like Robin Hood."

"Don't think it works like that," Cole said quietly, picking up a green tomato about the size of a baseball. "Last chance, go away."

"Hey, look at this!" was the last thing the thief said before a tomato hit him in the face. Before he could react, another one hit him in the same place.

The second boy held his hands up. "I surrender! Ain't no damn tomatoes worth this! Come on, Tommy, we need to go."

"Give me just a minute, I can't see. He's blinded me! I need to wipe these tomatoes out of my face."

It was the last Cole saw of them, but their excuse for stealing gave him an idea. He grabbed the basket, which the thieves had filled with tomatoes, beans, and corn, and carried it into the kitchen. Mrs. Wilson laughed and held up her hands. "Whoa! Stop! What are we going to do with all of this? Every inch of the closet and kitchen shelves are full of vegetables I've put up. We have more than enough food to get us through the winter and spring. I walked around the garden before you got here. I honestly think we've just scratched the surface."

"I might have an idea for that," Cole said. "What if we had a little fruit and vegetable stand? All it would take are a few boards and a hammer and nails, and I have a pretty good idea where I can get the lumber. We can make you a little money, especially if my dad tells the congregation about it."

"Well, it's a great idea," Mrs. Wilson said. "But who gets the money?"

Cole said quickly, "It's your money, your garden, you get the money."

"No, no. Cannot do it that way. We split it 50/50 or not at all. You've been much too good to me, and I want to share whatever we make with you."

"We don't have much fruit, but I know where we could purchase some peaches and apples and resell them in small baskets," Cole said.

Mrs. Wilson shook her head at Cole, smiling affectionately.

"When your father suggested you come and work with me, I had no idea it would turn out like this," Mrs. Wilson said. "At first, I was reluctant. I didn't really want another person hanging around the house. But, oh, my goodness! You're like part of my family. You take care of the money. I trust you."

A little startled by Mrs. Wilson's willingness to go along with his plan, Cole hesitated for a minute before he responded, "Well, your cornbread might be the answer. My friend Luther, wherever he is, seems to smell cornbread and greens whenever you're cooking. When he was here yesterday, he told me of a friend who has a large farm. He produces fruits and vegetables for sale in North Mississippi and West Tennessee. Luther says he would sell us as much as we could pay for. Right now, you have some cash saved up since most of your groceries came from the garden. If you will let me use that to buy peaches and watermelons, I believe we can double our money and then do it again."

"Better hurry. We have about a month, maybe six weeks, before the season is over. Get me some cucumbers, and I'll start making pickles to sell. James and Sarah can sit out there with their pet rabbit. James told me people were willing to pay a dollar for a picture of them holding Snake."

The little fruit and vegetable business worked like a dream. Every morning, either Cole or Britches would meet Luther's friend, who would sell them peaches, corn, and watermelons. Usually, they finished well before noon. James and Sarah helped every morning. One of them would hold the rabbit while the other helped with customers. Snake, the rabbit, preened from the attention he received.

As summer turned to fall, the supply of fruits and vegetables slowed down and finally stopped. Mrs. Wilson cooked an end-of-the-summer lunch of fried chicken and peach pie to celebrate the season. After lunch, she pulled out an old bank bag full of money.

"How much money do you think is in this, Cole?"

Before Cole could answer, Britches said, "A hundred dollars."

James and Sarah said, "No, way too high!"

And Cole said, "Three hundred dollars."

"None of you are even close; there is just over $2,400 in this bag. Cole, you take $1,200 as your half. I'll take care of James, Sarah, and Snake."

Somehow, they had run so fast buying and selling fruits and vegetables that they didn't have time to consider the profit they were making. Britches had worked with Cole half the time, and Luther had helped him start the garden and find a source of fruits and vegetables. When the garden played out, both Luther and Britches tried to refuse the money Cole gave them, but it was to no avail. Finally, they ended up celebrating with an apple pie that had just come out of the oven. In thinking about it, Cole would say it was one of the best days of his life, apple pie and peach pie all in the same day.

The best part of working with Mrs. Wilson was it did not interfere with baseball. For the most part, games were on weekends and practice was during the week. As the last player to join the team, Cole was the rookie and was rarely part of the starting lineup, unless someone was sick or out of town. Whenever there was an opening, Cole stepped in, mainly as an outfielder but once as a catcher.

It was in the playoffs at the end of the season when his star really began to shine. Two players in the starting lineup were home sick with the flu; one was a pitcher, and the other was a third baseman. The team played six games over the weekend, winning four and losing two, to finish in second place for the season. Not only did Cole win both games he pitched, but he also led the team in batting with more hits than any other player in the six games.

After one of the games Cole pitched, a stranger walked up to Cole and introduced himself as Bob Rogers, a college scout for the Mississippi State Bulldogs in Starkville. "Cole, I know college is still a few years away, but we would love for you to come visit us. Maybe see a game or two. Our program is at least as good as AA pro ball. I'll stay in touch."

Cole had stayed so busy taking care of Mrs. Wilson and playing travel ball that the prospect of playing professionally had not crossed his mind.

From that moment on, it was all he thought of.

Fruit & Vegetables

As winter approached, Cole continued to help Mrs. Wilson by chopping and splitting wood, not only for keeping the house warm but also for cooking. One day, she pulled him away from his chores. "Cole, go out to the garden and tell me what you see. Something strange is happening out there after dark, and it frightens me."

As Cole walked around the garden, he noticed little marks or holes in the ground about the size of a dime. On several of them, someone or something had made small excavations.

"Not sure what it is or who it is," Cole told Mrs. Wilson. "I guess the simplest thing to do is to get Britches to help me, and we'll sit up and watch. I'm sorry it is frightening you. We'll see if we can't solve the problem."

After going home for supper, the two boys returned to their vigil. After the house lights were turned off and Mrs. Wilson and the children went to bed, Cole and Britches took turns watching while the other napped.

Just before eleven, Britches grabbed Cole's shoulder to awaken him.

"It's—it's him, it's it or whatever it is!" Britches whispered. "I just saw him moving out there."

Cole was first out the door, waving a baseball bat. The heel of his shoe hung on the doorframe, and he went sailing out into the night, landing on his knees and elbows. Britches followed suit, falling over Cole and landing on top of him. To add to the chaos, Mrs. Wilson, who had been unable to sleep, came charging out the door in her nightgown, tripping over Britches and landing over Cole with her gown tangled around her.

The shadow in the garden stopped and came toward them. When a flashlight came on, a deep male voice said, "Oh, what a mess I have made."

Mrs. Wilson, frantically trying to get her nightgown down, yelled, "What in the hell are you doing in my garden in the middle of the night?"

"Let me introduce myself," the man said, holding up his hands to show he meant no harm. "My name is Mike Johnson. I apologize most heartily for this intrusion!"

Johnson was a member of the Mid-South Treasure Hunters Association, he told them. He'd been scouring maps and documents and scouting the area around the Wilsons' home. He was able to trace the former route of a train track that had been just south of the property. There once had been a small train station for shipping and receiving freight close to the Wilsons' property.

"In 1919, the year after Memphis was almost destroyed by the great influenza epidemic, there was a terrible train wreck just south of your garden," Johnson said. "The wreck caused a large fire, which consumed not only the train but the little station that sat here. Shortly after the accident, the track was abandoned, and the rails were pulled up for scrap. By 1930, there was no trace of either the station house or the track. But there is one more fact—that train was carrying a small safe full of money to pay the soldiers at Fort Jackson, South Carolina. It had over a half million dollars in gold coins that have never been found."

"What did the safe look like?" Mrs. Wilson asked.

"Just an iron box."

"Well, guess what? I may know where it is," Mrs. Wilson said. "When

Luther first broke up the garden, he found something like that. If you'll wait a minute, until I get a robe on, I'll show it to you. Cole, you know where it is. It's in the shed along with that piece of scrap metal."

Moments later, Cole and Britches dragged a rusty metal box to the front of the porch, where they turned it face up. A small brass tag on the front of the keyhole read, "Property of US Army." The safe door was rusted open, and the safe had been emptied of its contents long ago.

Now it was Mrs. Wilson's turn to talk.

"You can have the safe. I'll give you five minutes to get it out of my sight, and as for you, if I ever see you again anywhere near my property, you're going to hear a noise that sounds very much like a 12-gauge shotgun. The clock is ticking for you to start disappearing," she said bluntly. "Cole, you and Britches do what you want to with him if he's not gone in the next five minutes."

With that, Mrs. Wilson pulled her robe around her and marched back into the house. Two minutes later, Mr. Johnson was gone, having left the old safe behind.

Later, as the boys started home, Britches said, "Whew, that was a sight I'll long remember."

"That guy sneaking around in the garden?" Cole asked.

"No, I'm talking about Mrs. Wilson in her nightgown."

Cole's only response was, "Oh."

The next day, everything was back to normal. Fall and winter routines were settling in. Cole kept a large supply of wood near Mrs. Wilson's kitchen and did whatever else she needed. The incident of the nighttime treasure hunter was not mentioned again, though nobody involved was likely to forget it.

Later that morning, when things were quiet and the children were playing outside, Mrs. Wilson came and wrapped Cole in a fierce hug. She'd grown so fond of this young man and his friend, Britches. "I'm sorry about last night, but I was so worried about the two of you, I couldn't think straight. Cole, I simply could not let anything happen to you. You mean so much to us. Next time, I am going to stick the shotgun out the window and pull the trigger."

Realizing Mrs. Wilson was about to cry, Cole said, "Britches and I were proud of you. Now, I need to split a good bit of this wood."

"One last thing—I've been thinking about the money you gave me from the garden. Cole, if we do as good next year as we did this year, I'll have enough money for a new stove."

The next few years seemed to fly by. Between looking after Mrs. Wilson, going to school, and playing baseball in the summer, Cole had little time for anything else. Britches was on the same track. Even Socrates shared their baseball interest, shadowing the older boys until he joined a team and began playing with kids his own age.

One afternoon as Cole got ready to head over to Mrs. Wilson's house, his mother stopped him.

"Cole, where did you get those clothes? The shorts barely cover your knees, and your shirt is way too small. Have you grown that much, or are these somebody else's clothes?" Rachel asked her son, reaching to examine a loose button.

"No, Mom, I'm pretty sure they're mine. Same old clothes you used to see on my brothers before they got too big for them."

"Well, you come to the kitchen with me to where I can measure you." Near the back door on the inside of the closet was a marker where Cole, his brothers, and his sister had been measured. When his mother finished measuring him, she exclaimed, "Oh, my goodness, Cole, you've gone past your sister and almost caught your brothers. You've grown more than eight inches since I last measured you."

With Luther's help, Cole expanded the garden area where more vegetables and fruit could be grown. Mrs. Wilson had bought a new stove with the money made from the second year of gardening, and Cole could now spend some more time with the garden rather than splitting wood for the old stove.

Perhaps the biggest surprise of the summer came from Snake, the pet rabbit. One day, a second rabbit appeared, much to the twins' delight. Toward the end of the summer, Snake disappeared, only to reappear a week later with four tiny rabbits close behind.

Once again, the garden not only filled Mrs. Wilson's pantry but made an even larger profit than the year before. After splitting the money with Britches, Cole had enough to buy new clothes and nearly double the money he had in a savings account at the bank. If the garden did as well next year, he would be able to buy a used car.

Later, when he got home, his mother was waiting for him. "Cole, look at you! You look like a circus clown in those old clothes. I can alter some of your brothers' clothes to fit you."

"No, Mother. Thank you, but I don't want to do that. Those old clothes used to be Dad's. When he was finished with them, they were passed down to my brothers. Even after all this time, they still smell like cigar smoke. And more than that, they look like a preacher's clothes. I'm not a preacher. Not headed that way. Doubt if I ever will be. Thank you for your help, but with your permission, I plan to take a small part of my garden money to go and buy some new clothes."

To Cole's surprise, his mother agreed. "You're right, Cole. Perhaps I've been blind. You're not a little boy any longer. I couldn't see it, but you're grown up now. Let's go get you some new clothes."

As Cole began his last year in high school, he had a hard time keeping his mind on his schoolwork. Every week, someone from a different college would call or visit, trying to sell him on their baseball program. Britches, who'd become a fine player in his own right, was beginning to draw his own share of attention from colleges.

As time allowed, Cole visited most of the schools in the Southeastern Conference, along with two schools in Missouri and one in New Orleans. Mississippi State and Bob Rogers had been the first to contact Cole, and in the end, they would be his best move.

When, at last, high school athletes could accept scholarships from teams at the college of their choice, Cole's friends expected him to choose Tennessee or Ole Miss. Instead, he and Britches once again wound up on the same team, at Mississippi State University in Starkville.

Property of
U.S.ARMY

It was midway through a Mississippi State game against the South Carolina Gamecocks, and Cole sat on the bench struggling to keep his eyes open. He had been up late the night before studying for a chemistry test, and staying awake was all he could do. Besides, he had pitched yesterday—pitched well—allowing only two hits in five innings.

To stay awake, Cole began thinking back about his first days in college. He had been recruited by at least twenty schools that offered him full baseball scholarships. Mississippi State had been after him since his early days in travel ball and had convinced him that the Bulldogs would offer his best chance to be drafted high by a major league team. Now he was midway through his senior year in college, and the major league draft of 1997 was not far away.

As a college athlete, Cole had arrived almost ten days before the rest of the freshman class. When the other students arrived, the dorms looked like a three-ring circus with students struggling to carry large bags. Amid the chaos, several fraternities cooked hamburgers and hot dogs while two sororities passed out water and lemonade.

Several members of the baseball team had a large sign advertising the "RW&B Fund." For an appropriate contribution, they would help move bags and appliances into the dorms. When the day was over, Cole had collected more than a hundred dollars. (Few people ever realized that the RW&B fund stood for Red Wine & Beer!)

Cole did not receive much playing time until midseason of his freshman year. At first, the coaches tried to change his delivery, but they soon gave up when they realized how hard he was throwing. Later in the season, Cole moved up to become one of the starting pitchers, and he continued to start throughout his sophomore, junior, and now into his senior year. He was the team's top pitcher. Cole planned to declare himself for the draft after completing his career at Mississippi State.

But the next week, during a game against Georgia, everything changed.

Parts of the incident he could remember; fortunately, some parts were hidden from him. It was spring, a perfect baseball afternoon. Cole was pitching well—at the top of his game. Today was an important conference game, but the major league draft was fast approaching. Cole had a lot to think about, but for the moment, he just needed to get the next batter out. It didn't happen that way.

The batter swung and hit a line drive right back at him. As Cole raised his hands to protect himself, the ball struck him in the right eye.

He knew he was hurt, probably badly. His hand went to his face, his eye, and he could feel blood, a lot of it. He could sense people running to him, some already standing around him. Within minutes, an ambulance was on the field, and then he was on the way to the emergency room.

When it was all over, Cole would always remember a doctor telling him he'd been lucky.

"It was a glancing blow on the side of your eye and not direct. Could have cost you an eye, but I think we're going to be okay," the doctor told him. "Not going to look real pretty for a week or so. Some black and a little blue, but a lot of purple for a week at least. You're going to have to rest for a couple of weeks and no baseball for a while. An ophthalmologist will need to look at it as soon as the blood in the eye clears up. Another thing, you're going to stay with us for two or three days so we can keep an eye on you—make sure nothing else turns up. Use common sense; you've had a severe injury. You badly need to rest, and it looks like your teammates are waiting to see you."

Britches was the first person Cole saw, followed by most of the team, still in their uniforms.

"Boy, you scared me to death. I thought it knocked your eye out," Britches said when he came into the room. "You'd better call your mom. She's worried sick."

"Well, I'm okay," Cole said. "Pretty numb right now and a little sick at my stomach. Sorta mad at myself. I should have never tried to get him out with a curveball; a fastball would've done it for sure. Tell everybody I'm okay. I'll be out of here in a day or two and be back on the team by next week."

That was the last thing he remembered until he woke up the next morning.

Two days later, Cole left the hospital with a patch over his eye and an appointment with the ophthalmologist in a week. In the immediate future, rest and no baseball were prescribed. It was as if he had been on a train that suddenly stopped in the middle of nowhere. What could he do? The answer was nothing but watch other people do things.

The week dragged by, and finally he went to see the ophthalmologist, Dr. Tracey Livingston. When the doctor walked into the examining room, to Cole's surprise, he met an attractive young woman.

"Here's the baseball player I keep hearing about. Let's take a look at that eye and see how it's coming," she said.

"My eye is fine. I can see just fine, and I'm ready to go back to the team," Cole replied.

Ignoring him, the doctor said, "I'm going to take a look as soon as you sit down in that chair." The tone of her voice made it evident who was in charge. Cole sat down and let her remove the bandage and the patch.

"The first thing I'm going to tell you is you were lucky. Whatever you do, avoid another injury to this area," Dr. Livingston said.

"Doctor, I did not plan on this, and I promise not to do it again," Cole replied.

"I'm sure you didn't, but let me see. You still have some blood in the eye, but I suspect that will clear itself up. The one thing we want to watch is the pressure in the eye. Typically, it is higher than normal after an injury like this, and it is. I want to watch that and make sure it comes down. You do not want to be worried at this point about glaucoma, which could cause permanent injury or sight loss. I want to see you in three weeks, and take it easy. No baseball."

When Cole left the office, he found Britches waiting outside.

"What did she say? Did she turn you loose to come back to the team? Woodson's a great pitcher, but he's not you."

"No, looks like I won't be coming right back. That woman must have just gotten out of the Marine Corps. Maybe I can be back in time for the playoffs."

Three days later, against the doctor's orders, Cole decided to give it a try. He got Britches to come with him, and they walked to an empty baseball diamond behind the stadium where nobody could see them. At first, Cole threw a few easy pitches, just happy to be there. His next three pitches sailed over Britches's head.

"You okay? I've never seen you do that before."

"No, I'm not. Dammit. I'm not. I can't see you. At first I could, but now you're all fuzzy. Can't really pitch if I can't see the batter. Maybe in a week or so."

After a week, they tried again, but the result was the same. There was nothing else to do but wait.

Two weeks later, when Dr. Livingston walked into the room, Cole knew from the look on her face that she did not have good news.

"Cole, I'm sorry. I had hoped for good news, but it was not to be," she said. "The pressure in your eye has gone up instead of down. I'm going to double the medicine you're taking in hopes that will help. Instead of one drop twice a day, I'm going to change the prescription to two drops twice a day. I'm hoping we can control this with medicine instead of surgery."

Cole was disappointed, but the news was not unexpected. He trusted that his long-term prognosis was still good.

"Instead of giving me bad news, why not give me something positive to think about?" Cole changed the subject. "Will you go out to dinner with me?"

"No, I will not go out with you. I'm way too old, and you are way too young," the doctor said, softening the rejection with a smile. Then, with a twinkle in her eye, she added, "Get that pressure down in your eye, and maybe I'll give it further consideration."

Eye Injury Threatens Baseball Career

Cole is hit in the eye by a line drive that, although serious, seems to be temporary. It is only discovered later that the force of the trauma has caused glaucoma. Glaucoma is a disease of the eye that results in a buildup of pressure within the eyeball that can damage the optic nerve and lead to blindness. Glaucoma can have many causes, including age, diabetes, and traumatic injury. It can be controlled with eyedrops, laser treatment, and surgery to drain fluid out of the eye.

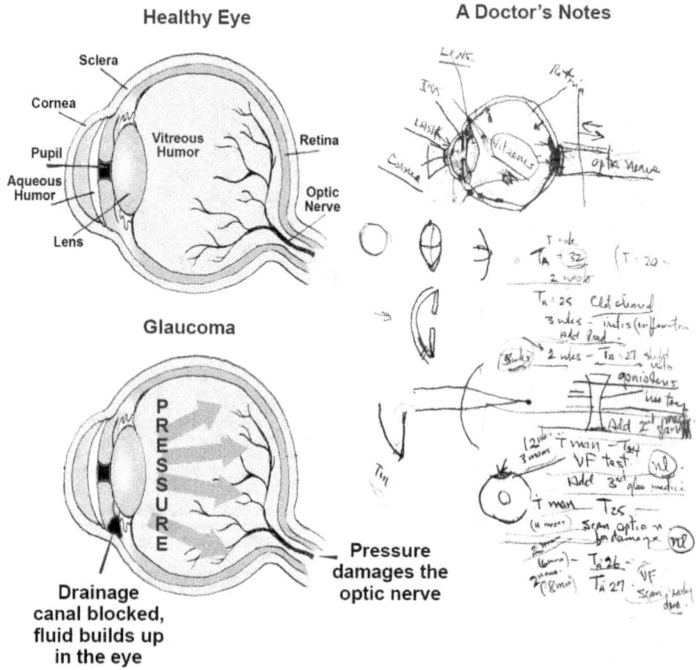

Two more weeks had passed, and it was time for Cole to see Dr. Livingston again. After a brief conversation, it was obvious she did not have a positive report.

"Well, I'm sad to say today I only have bad news for you," the doctor said.

The increase in drops did not help Cole's eye pressure as they'd hoped. The pressure had even gone up a bit. Dr. Livingston had also found a small tear in his retina. Surgery was his only option.

"Chances are that surgery can fix the problem, and your vision will be normal," she said. She chuckled and added, "After you recover and you have good eyesight, you will see that I'm not near as pretty as you think I am. However, if your offer is still good, I will go out to dinner with you."

"Sounds like I won the battle and lost the war. How long does it take to recover from something like this?" Cole asked.

"Your vision will come back quickly. That's what this is all about. But there will be no baseball or strenuous activity for three months."

"I can take the news about the surgery. I accept that as necessary, but the three months of recovery kills me. If I'm figuring right, that means I can't pitch until August. I will have graduated by then and not only will college be behind me, but so will any chance of ever playing professional baseball," Cole said, deflated, as the realization began to sink in. "You've got to understand where I'm coming from; I don't want to sound ungrateful. I have a wonderful family. My dad is a preacher. My two brothers are preachers, and my sister is a church secretary. I'm the last piece to the puzzle. Maybe, possibly, someday, I might become a preacher, but not now. I'm an athlete, a baseball pitcher. I'm sorry. I know it's not your job to listen to sob stories, but I wasn't expecting this. Is there any other way?"

"No, Cole," Dr. Livingston said. "There's no other way. I suppose you could wear a patch over your eye, sort of like a pirate, or you could lose sight in your eye. That's not what you want. The lab results don't lie. You have serious problems in that eye, and it has got to be corrected. You know I'm an eye doctor, not a guidance counselor, but I bet your career is just beginning, not ending. Whatever lies ahead for you, let's get this problem fixed, and then you can see what the next steps will be."

With another week to go before the surgery, Cole was left with little to do but study. He was close to graduating from college, and good grades could only improve his chances for admission to graduate school—if he chose to go.

On the first day of May, as directed, Cole checked himself into the hospital. By midmorning, his surgery was over, and Cole was in recovery. The operation had gone smoothly, and hopefully the problem was corrected. Dr. Livingston came in to see him shortly after he awoke.

"How's my patient? Your procedure went perfectly, and I expect good news from your lab reports. How are you feeling?"

"I have to admit, it was pretty easy. The worst thing was checking in at 3:30 a.m. How long will I have this patch over my eye, and when do I get to take you to dinner?"

"We'll see about that in a few weeks, after I see your reports. You go back to sleep. I have six other patients to see about, but remember, you're my favorite."

A minute later, there was a knock on the door, and Cole's father, Dan, and brother Bill came in.

"Well, dang, if I had a doctor who looked like that, I might consider having surgery," Bill grinned.

"Yeah, she's pretty special, says I can take her out to dinner when this is all over."

"Just get better and get this behind you," Cole's father said. "When you get out in two days, I want to drive you home. Mom's worried sick over you, and we need to spend some time together."

To Cole's disappointment, Dr. Livingston was absent two days later when he was discharged from the hospital. A male nurse brought his discharge papers along with a note from her saying, "Sorry to miss you. See you in two weeks. Take it easy until then."

It was good to be back home where he could rest and recover under his mother's watchful eye. One afternoon, he went to see Pearly and Luther. If by chance Pearly had a fresh-baked pie around, he felt sure it would be good for his eye. After handshakes and hugs, Pearly said, "Sorta guessed you might come see us."

"What's that I smell? Pearly, what are you hiding?"

"Well, you've been gone so long, I forgot how to make pies anymore. I did get a cherry pie that might taste all right if we put a couple scoops of ice cream on it."

"My eye is feeling better already," Cole said.

They caught up on family news over their pie. Luther and Pastor Dan had gone golfing the other day and had run into some of the dads from Cole's old travel team. Socrates was still playing ball for his high school, and Luther thought he might land some scholarship offers.

Then Luther asked a question for which Cole had no answer. "What are you planning on doing with yourself now that your schooling is over? You going to follow your dad? Be a preacher man?"

"Don't really know. Wish I did. Before I got hurt, I had hoped to be a ballplayer."

"Mm-hmm. Uh-huh," was all Luther had to say. Perhaps he would have said more, but Pearly looked at him and shook her head.

After Cole had gone, Pearly cornered Luther. "I know what you was fixing to ask him. About playing professional baseball. Certainly his papa'll be hoping he's going to be a preacher. Wouldn't that be something, all four of them being preachers at the same time? Be quite a sight."

The next morning at breakfast, Cole's father asked, "What plans do you have for the day? I would love to take you to my office, walk around the church, show you what I do, and meet some of the people I work with."

This came as no surprise; after all, despite his injury, Cole would be graduating from college at the end of the summer term, and just having graduated from college didn't entitle one to sit around doing nothing.

Cole spent the next day meeting the church staff members and shadowing his father. Though he was doing this as a favor to his parents, somewhat to his surprise, he enjoyed the day. Perhaps ministry was the career he should pursue, but he wasn't ready to commit to three or four more years of schooling. He would have to think about that.

When Cole returned to school, it was time for the follow-up examination on his eye and to see Dr. Livingston again. When he entered the doctor's office, the smile on her face told him she had good news.

"I could not be more pleased with the results," she said. "The pressure on your eye is almost back to normal. I honestly think your eye is looking so much better than I had expected or even hoped for. Even though you are doing well, your eye still needs rest. No baseball or sports of any type until the first of August."

Though Cole had been expecting the news of no baseball for three months, the finality of it was just sinking in. No. More. Baseball. Probably time to think about taking a different path. Somehow, he had hoped something would change, but it had not.

It wasn't all bad news that day, however. The doctor offered to take him to dinner.

Dinner with Tracey Livingston was awkward, restrained, and wonderful. She was the most striking woman in the restaurant. Cole was thinking of ways to keep the relationship alive when she reached across the table and said, "I need to tell you something."

"Okay."

"I'm too old for you. Wish I weren't, but I am. You would be easy for me to fall for, but I don't think it's something I should do."

"Well," Cole said, "I don't agree. I may be young, younger than you, but I'm bigger. I'm almost six foot five inches tall. What I propose is that we drink the rest of our bottle of wine."

"I accept your proposal," she replied, and then the scene abruptly changed.

An older man sitting at the next table stood and came over to them. "Pardon me, did I just hear you propose to this lovely young lady? I say we should all congratulate this young couple."

With that, other couples around them began calling, "Toast! Toast! Kiss the bride!"

As other couples stood and began toasting them, Cole decided to respond in some fashion. Raising his glass in a toast, he leaned across the table and kissed the bride. Just as surprised as he was, she threw her arms around him and kissed him back!

"Here's my toast, Tracey," he whispered. "Here's to someday."

"I'll toast to that," she replied and kissed him again. "Now you need to take the bride home. I've got surgery tomorrow starting at six in the morning."

When he dropped her off, she kissed him goodnight and said, "I hadn't planned on getting married, but the evening was quite an adventure. Call me in a day or so, and I'll buy you lunch."

And so, the courtship that had begun as a joke continued until one day in early July when Tracey called and said they needed to talk. Sensing something was wrong, he met her after work.

"Let's walk. I need to tell you something."

"I don't feel so good about this," said Cole, sensing bad news.

"Both good and bad. I've been offered a fellowship in Boston—a research clinic that deals with injuries to the eye. It's a dream job. I'm very fond of you, and I've dreaded telling you this." When there was no response, she said, "Are you okay?"

"Well, I'm thinking about throwing up," he mumbled. "Guess I should say, 'Congratulations, I'm proud of you,' but I'm sad. I'm not sure where we were headed; now I guess we're not headed anywhere."

"I know, I know. I didn't know where we were headed either. I'm not at all sure what the future holds for either of us. Maybe it will be special someday. Maybe someday."

Two weeks later, Tracey was gone to Boston, which seemed as far away as if it were another country. Left behind and feeling sorry for himself, Cole had little to do but study for final exams and graduate from college. But still, as he studied, he could not forget the last time he saw her, when she kissed him goodbye and whispered, "Maybe someday." Summer term exams were soon over, followed by graduation, and then his college days were but a memory.

A week after graduation, while sitting at home, Cole reflected that most college graduates would be celebrating; not so for him. At a loss for what to do next, he looked at his options. The obvious choice was to begin down the path of becoming a preacher. It would mean three years, perhaps even four years, of graduate school, which was not a very appealing choice for now.

Knowing his family was watching to see what "little brother" was going to do, he took a temporary job in a sporting goods store—the same place where he had bought his baseball glove years ago.

Late one afternoon after work, he stopped by Luther's house, mainly to see if Pearly had any cake or pie that needed eating. It had been nearly a month since Cole had seen them, and there was much to talk about. After the obligatory talk about Cole's recovery from the eye injury, there was an awkward silence. After a bit, Luther looked at Pearly and she said, "Go ahead, you've been busting to ask him."

Knowing what was coming, Cole jumped in. "What am I doing next? I don't really know, been filling out forms for graduate school, different schools, different places. Trying to get comfortable with going back to school for three or four years. Do preachers get free cake and pie?"

Luther, as always, wasted no time in responding, "It'd be good. Your papa being such a fine preacher, your two brothers now preaching, and here come you. What a bunch of preachers! It's unusual; can't think of anything quite like it. That'd be very nice, just fine. Let me ask you one question, though. Has something happened I didn't know about? Has your arm fallen off?"

"I guess you're talking about me playing baseball. I had sort of moved on past it. Feels like I missed my chance. It was my dream since I was a little boy, but time moved on."

After a long silence, Luther surprised Cole by asking, "You want to see? To make sure? I once thought you had a pretty good shot at the big leagues. Might be nice to see if you're good enough."

"I'm all right with preaching, but do you know something? Tell me what you're hinting at."

"A friend of mine asked about you. Saw you pitch a year or two ago. Wanted to take a look at you."

"Why me? Is he a scout or something?"

"He's a good friend, used to be a teammate in the old days. Been a scout for years for the Cardinals."

Warming up to the idea, Cole asked, "What would I have to do?"

"A week from today, he's going to be in Medina about an hour from here, right out of Humboldt. All you need to do is show up and see if that's something you would like to do."

"It's been over four months since I even picked up a baseball. Doubt if I would be very good."

"Ain't but one way to find out. Go home and think about it," Luther advised.

"You got any suggestions about how to tell my dad I'm thinking about playing baseball rather than preaching?" Cole asked.

"Expect you might be surprised. We've been friends a very long time. He wants whatever is best for you. Go see."

Not feeling very good about the outcome, Cole decided to wait until after supper to bring it up. When he did, his father's response was not what he expected: "The Cardinals? The St. Louis Cardinals? Wouldn't have expected them to be so close to home. Would've expected it to be the Cubs or the Browns. Give it a try. See what you can do."

Feeling relieved and suddenly happy with the prospect, Cole went to the empty lot behind the church the next morning. Little had changed in the past few years, except the grass was knee-high. His target, a tin pie plate, was still on a log where he'd nailed it years ago. The old trail at the back of the lot, the one Britches used to come through, was still there. But that was a scene from the past, and Britches had just been drafted by the Detroit Tigers.

After cutting the grass, Cole dragged out the old sack of baseballs and started throwing at the pie pan. At first, he was awful, no control and very little speed. Biting his lip, he resolved, "I could do this once; I can do it again."

By the end of the third day, Cole was getting better. Each day, he improved until he felt like he was close to where he had been before he was injured. When it came to the tryouts, he was content with the feeling that he was ready. If he did well, he would play baseball; if not, he would move on with plans to be a preacher.

When Cole arrived, he was surprised to find nearly a hundred people standing around, waiting for instructions. An older man who was in charge began separating players by position. There were at least twenty pitchers, some of whom appeared to be in high school and some who looked to be five to ten years older than Cole. Each pitcher had a chance to throw twenty-five to thirty pitches to one of the catchers, with one of the coaches holding a speed gun.

When it was Cole's turn, the coach stopped him after five pitches. "Let's let you save that," he said. "Speed gun has you at about 100. We'll let you rest until we have a chance to look at some of these other pitchers."

Cole sat on the tailgate of a truck for a little while. An hour later, one of the coaches called for him. "Coach wants to talk to you. He's in the stands over there, behind home plate."

When Cole reached home plate, he saw an older black man wearing a

Cardinals cap. He was almost a carbon copy of Luther. At the moment, he was on the phone.

"Pretty big crowd. Not much here, though. Couple of kids might be okay. One big outfielder looks like a football player and one kid, shortstop, is a real prospect. I'll try to sign him and maybe the big outfielder, but there's one more, a pitcher, an old friend wants me to look at. I'll let you know later today."

Ending the call, he looked at Cole and laughed. "Lord, Lord! Now what is Luther wasting my time with today, and how is my old friend? He still hanging on to Pearly, I hope? Now tell me about your eye, can you see real good? Might be a good thing having a one-eyed pitcher—scare batters to death! Now, I'm going to quit talking and give you a chance."

For the next five minutes, Cole described the injury to his eye as well as he could. He also talked about before he was hurt, and his hopes to be drafted by a major league team.

"I understand that, but now tell me this, are you right-handed or left-handed?"

"I'm right-handed, but I throw left-handed. I expect Luther explained that to you."

"Which he did, I just needed to hear you say it, and it's the first time I've seen it," the coach said. "I tell you what, we've talked enough; go out on the mound and let me watch you. See what you can do."

After just a few minutes, the coach yelled, "That's enough! Seen all I need to see. Figured Luther wouldn't have called me if you weren't good. Now this is what I can offer, don't have no options, only this: The Cardinals will offer you a one-time bonus of $40,000. That's the best I can do. You would go into the rookie league in Johnson City, Tennessee.

"Depending on how you do, you could get promoted to Class A ball in Peoria, Illinois, or a set higher to Palm Beach. The ladder gets pretty steep after that; AA is in Springfield, Missouri, and AAA is Memphis, Tennessee. Of course, after that is St. Louis and the major leagues.

"You have three days to decide. If you accept, you would need to go to Johnson City for rookie ball next June. You would be a real hit in East

Tennessee. Folks there have never seen a pitcher who used to be right-handed, and now he's a southpaw. They are good people. They'll fatten you up on turnip greens and cornbread, teach you to love chitlins."

"Not real sure what that is, but I like collard greens," Cole replied. "Taste a lot like grass to me."

"I would like to take a day to talk to my parents. Thank you for the offer."

The drive home gave Cole time to plan how to tell his parents and exactly what to tell them. In a way, he would be disappointing them if he accepted the offer. Maybe it would be best to go to graduate school and start on the path to be a preacher. But was that what he wanted or what they wanted?

Cole went back and forth worrying until he realized he was sitting in the car outside his house. Hoping to avoid his parents, he entered the house through the back door, where he ran straight into his mother.

"Whoa, you scared me! You okay? You don't look so good. Did you get bad news at the tryouts?"

"In fact, they made me an offer, and I had planned to tell you about it later," Cole replied.

"Don't keep me standing here; what did they offer?"

"They offered me $900 a month for the first season, and a $40,000 bonus. I would start in a rookie league in Johnson City." At first, his mother didn't respond, just stood there; then tears began to run down her cheeks as she wrapped her arms around him.

"Mama, don't cry; I haven't accepted the offer," Cole said.

"No, no," she stammered. "I'm so excited. Just caught me by surprise; $40,000, that's more than your father makes in a year. Remember, I've already got three sons and a husband who are preachers, and it's about time for a baseball player."

Later that afternoon, when Cole's father came home from work at the church, he appeared to be deep in thought.

"You okay, Dad?"

"Oh, yeah. I'm fine," his father replied. "Just struggling with a sermon that won't come together, and the presbytery executive is due here Sunday.

How did the tryouts go? I expect that's why I'm having trouble with the sermon; my mind's been on baseball. And why does your mother keep peeking around the door? Have you got something to tell me?"

"Yes, sir. I got an offer from the Cardinals to play rookie ball. Start off in Johnson City, $900 a month in salary, and a signing bonus of $40,000." Cole paused. "And Dad, I'll do what you say. Should I go to graduate school or go play ball?"

"You want me to make the decision? I can do that. Have you got that fellow's phone number? How long have you got? What if he changes his mind or runs out of money? I say yes. Do it, do it, do it now. My prayers have been answered! I am so very proud of you. Have you told Luther yet? We can go over there later and give him the news."

A few minutes later, with both parents listening, Cole dialed the number of the Cardinals coach. On the fourth ring, a gruff voice answered, "Coach Ralston here."

"Hey, Coach. This is Cole Adams. Is that offer still on the table?"

"Yes, it is. You ready to pitch for the Cardinals?"

"Yes, sir!" was all Cole managed to say.

"Well, tell you what, I'll make it easy for you. I'm on my way now to visit with my old teammate, Luther, and maybe get a piece of Pearly's strawberry pie. If you're okay with that, I'll meet you there in an hour."

An hour later, there wasn't much room left in Pearly's kitchen with Luther and Coach Ralston joined by Cole, his parents, his brothers Bill and Joseph, his sister Cecile, and Socrates. Luther and Coach Ralston were telling stories about their time together as teammates. Rising to the occasion, Pearly produced not one but two strawberry pies to celebrate the event. Luther produced something in a large, dusty bottle.

Cole declined at first, before noticing both of his parents and his brothers were enjoying whatever it was. Not wanting to miss the fun, Cole soon had a glass of his own. Coach Ralston pulled out a contract and a check.

After Cole signed the contract, the coach proposed a toast, saying, "Congratulations, Cole! You are now the property of the St. Louis Cardinals. May you be as good as we think you are."

Cecile asked, "Where will he go? Will he be in St. Louis, and can we watch him on television?"

"Well, he'll be pitching for the Cardinals, all right, but it's not St. Louis, it's Johnson City in East Tennessee," Coach Ralston said. "That is where the lion's share of our rookies start out. They will be playing against other rookies from major league teams. Some players will move up the ladder to other teams; hopefully, some will play in the major leagues one day."

More toasts followed. A few minutes later, a reporter from the local newspaper arrived to take a picture of Cole holding his bonus check and wearing a brand-new Cardinals hat. When Luther's bottle was empty and the party began to break up, all three preachers stood up and said they had sermons to work on, and Cole's sister had to work in the morning.

By the time Cole left, Luther and Coach Ralston had found something else to drink and were reliving their days in the minor leagues. The next morning, it was obvious that the wine, or whatever it was Luther had served, had both families moving slowly and a bit out of step.

Cole's first stop that day was to find Britches Malone, his companion and catcher during the time Cole was learning to pitch left-handed. Britches had signed a minor-league contract with the Detroit Tigers but was at home for a few weeks recovering from a wrist injury. Upon hearing the news that Cole had signed a contract with the Cardinals, Britches immediately said, "Let's go celebrate!"

"Uh, oh," Cole replied. "We went over to Luther's last night to meet the coach and sign the contract. Luther produced some kind of wine that tasted better last night than it does this morning. Let's go over to the boxing club; I need to tell them about it."

When they got to the gym, they found Cole's old nemesis, Robert Sullivan, skipping rope and punching a bag. Long ago, Robert had bullied Cole, knocking him down and hurting his right arm. After Cole had evened the score, an awkward friendship had developed.

"Hey, Cole, I hear you got a contract to play ball with the Cardinals. Congratulations!" Robert said. "Glad to hear it. And Britches, you're playing in the American League in the Tigers' chain. Hard to believe two of our old group are playing professional ball."

Cole responded, "What about you, Robert? How's the fighting coming along?"

"Funny you would ask. Just got word this morning, I have a fight lined up in Hawaii, end of the summer. It will be my third fight, undefeated—so far—and thanks to you for introducing me to Luther and these people here at the gym. Looking back, who could have seen this? Two playing professional baseball and the other a professional boxer."

The next spring, as Cole finished packing and prepared to leave, he recalled the magic of Robert's statement at the boxing club. From such an improbable beginning, the three of them were on their way. Tucked in Cole's pocket was a letter he had received the day after he signed his contract. He read it for the thirty-fifth time; it was only three lines:

Proud of you.
Miss you and think of you all the time.
Who knows? Maybe someday.

"Maybe someday" was the way Tracey had always ended their communications, and who knows, maybe someday.

Telling his parents goodbye, Cole was surprised to see Luther in the yard with Pearly waving a sign. On one side, it read, "Hurry back!" and on the other, it said, "Go Cardinals!"

Feeling more than a little emotional, Cole turned left out of his old street and headed south. Just out of town, he pulled over and looked back, and a wave of homesickness swept over him. He could still turn around and go back. It would be embarrassing at first, but after a week or so, they would laugh and say, "Remember when you almost pitched for the St. Louis Cardinals?"

Knowing he would never have another chance like this, he pulled back on the road and started driving.

7

By late afternoon, Cole had reached the edge of Johnson City. Not sure what to do or where to go, he decided to find the ballpark and stopped for directions at a gas station. When he found the ballpark, a large sign at the entrance read, "Johnson City, Tennessee: Gateway to the St. Louis Cardinals."

Walking out on the field, he was startled to hear, "Hey, Cole. Glad you're here. Been wondering when you might arrive." An older man in a worn Cardinals jersey walked up, asking, "You ready to pitch?"

"I'm ready to go!" Cole responded with a wide grin.

"I'm Coach Montague," the older man said, smiling. "Most people call me Smokey. That's Coach Nichols over there by the dugout. He will show you the fraternity house across the street where most of the team stays. Practice is tomorrow at nine. You will get a uniform then."

In a few minutes, Coach Nichols came over, introduced himself, and asked if Cole wanted to see the frat house at East Tennessee State University.

"Let's go take a look," Cole responded. "I lived in a fraternity house at Starkville for four years, so this should be easy enough." The ETSU frat house was empty during the summer, which made it easy for the baseball team.

"Rent is $100 a month and includes all-you-can-eat breakfast," Coach Nichols said. "It is payable in advance, or they can deduct it from your paycheck. I'll give you the rental agreement tomorrow. Remember, practice tomorrow at nine, and a little hint, Coach really likes to start about ten minutes early."

After Coach Nichols had left, Cole started moving into his new room. *How strange! Not so long ago, I was packing up to leave a fraternity house in Mississippi and now here I am again.* In his room, over his bed, was a sign that read, "East Tennessee State University: Home of the Buccaneers." *Looks like I'm going to be a Buccaneer for a little while. Guess that's okay, but it seems like a long way from St. Louis.*

The next morning, just about eight thirty, Cole was standing on the baseball field along with thirty other players.

"Okay, men, listen up," Coach Montague said. "I'm going to break you up by position. First group is pitchers and catchers; Coach Nichols will be your pitching coach. Coach Johnson there, the outfield. And you infielders are lucky; you got me. First, let me congratulate you. You are no longer amateurs. You are professional baseball players. This is something you can tell your grandchildren, that you once played professional baseball in the St. Louis Cardinals system. This is rookie ball, the first rung on the ladder that could take you all the way to St. Louis. You have sixty days to prove yourself. You will be here for just over eight weeks. We will play four games a week and practice on the other days. The bad news is many of you will not move up to the next level. We will, however, try to help you to do so. Coaches will take you by the supply room to get your uniforms, and the good news is you get to keep them. Now, go. Pitchers first, get going."

For the next four days, the players worked with a coach. In Cole's group, there were nine other pitchers from all over the country, though many of them were from the deep South. Cole's accent made him stick out, and a lot of the players teased him, calling him "Memphis." The coaches worked them in pairs, and Cole was paired with a boy from deep in Georgia. Cole nicknamed him "Possum."

By day four, each pitcher was to pitch for four innings or thirty minutes.

"What are we supposed to do in this batting practice? Are we supposed to get them out?" Cole asked.

"Why don't you just relax and let them hit?" Coach Nichols quipped.

"Not me. I didn't come here to throw batting practice."

Smiling, the coach handed him the ball. "Strike 'em all out, Memphis. Let's see what you got."

Thirty minutes later, Cole was finished, having struck out nine and allowed only three routine groundballs. "Nice start, Cole. Someone will look at some film. If we can change or vary your delivery, you'll be able to keep the hitters out and off the bases."

One of the opposing batters walked over and said, "Hey, Coach, we need to get rid of this guy. He's bad for us."

Laughing, Coach Nichols said, "What's the matter?"

"Well, the problem is we can't hit what we can't see. He has an unusual delivery, almost sidearm, and the batter doesn't see the ball until it's almost too late."

"One thing for sure, Cole, we're not going to let you pitch to the Cardinals rookies anymore," the coach said. "If we did, I'm afraid none of them would get out of rookie ball. Tell me a secret. All our scanning reports on you showed your fastball. Where did your sidearm delivery come from?"

"Long time ago, when I was a kid, I got in a fight with the town bully. I got beat up pretty good—hurt my right arm and pulled something on my side—couldn't throw anymore. So I switched and taught myself to throw left-handed. I was still a little sore, so I dropped my delivery down around my knees. Been that way ever since, even after my right side healed."

"If I thought I could throw like you do, I might break my right arm and try the other," said a big redheaded boy from Georgia.

The routine stayed the same for the next two weeks of pitching five innings every fourth day. At the beginning of the third week, Coach Nichols took the ten pitchers into one of the training rooms where a camera and screen were set up.

"Let's look at the numbers first, and then we'll look at some film. Based on past experience, I can tell you only three of you—maybe four—will advance to low A ball in Peoria, Illinois, or high A in Palm Beach. Nothing personal—that's just the way it works out, entirely based on your performance. One or two will make it to AA in Springfield, Missouri, and that may be the highest anybody goes. AAA is in Memphis and is a long way from here, and of course, there is St. Louis at the end of the track. The purpose of this talk is to tell you about reality and how you might advance up the ladder.

"Now, I'm going to get specific and talk about each of you. Cole, you were the first to pitch, so I'm going to talk about you and then go in the order the other nine of you followed. Cole, in every game you pitched, the results are similar. Lights out in the first inning; the hitters are fooled by your delivery. They don't pick up the pitch, and your fastball overcomes them. Notice, however, the strikeouts go away after the first three innings. They've seen you now and know what to expect. You only throw fastballs, keep the ball inside, and they begin to hit you. Change pitches, change speeds, and change locations if you want to have a chance to move up. The batters you face are on the same program as you. They either go up or go home—it's tough, but it works. You will get another four or five weeks. Do your best and work on what I told you."

Later, sitting in his room, Cole began to face reality that he might not move up with the Cardinals. It sure had been easy for him—all the way back to travel ball. What if he got cut and didn't move up to A ball in Florida? What if he had to go home and tell people he didn't make it? That thought remained with him through a restless night and into practice the next day.

Cole was scheduled to pitch against a Philadelphia rookie league team in two days. Though he had not seen these players yet, they had the best record of anyone in the league. Two of their outfielders were leading the league in batting average and home runs. There was little doubt the coaches would be watching the next day. After yesterday's lecture, Cole knew he'd better mix up his pitches and change his routine. When the afternoon was over, Cole had only allowed three hits in five innings and no runs. He had done so by mixing up pitching and speeds with a few fastballs.

That game marked a change in his progress, and he seemed to improve each time he pitched. As the end of the two-month season approached, Cole felt like it was exam day in college when they would get their final grades. Already, four of the players had retired and were sent home. If Cole did not move up, a move to Alaska might be better than going home.

One by one, the players were called into the manager's office. The pitchers were the last to be called. It was a scene reminiscent of long ago when Cole had failed to make his Little League team. As his thoughts revolved around the disaster of that day, a coach brought him back to reality when he yelled, "Okay, Adams, Coach wants to see you."

When Cole walked into the small office, Coach stood up with a smile. "You ready to get some sand in your shoes? Real proud of your progress. You came a long way in a very short time."

Two days later, Cole had packed, said his goodbyes, and left for Florida, home of the Palm Beach Cardinals. With only six weeks left in the season, he understood the urgent need to contribute to a team fighting for the league championship. When he reached the stadium, the lights were out except for a few at the entrance. A guard stepped out of the shadows. "Ain't no game tonight! Reckon you could figure that out by yourself."

"I'm not here to watch a game. I'm a player. When will they be back?" Cole asked.

"Back sometime tonight. Be after midnight. You Adams? If you are, Manager Whitsel left you a note."

The note was simple and to the point:

Welcome to Florida. Team is in Miami for a game tonight. Practice tomorrow afternoon at two o'clock. Be here at one to get your uniform. Game tomorrow is at seven o'clock versus Miami—you're pitching.

Whitsel

A little before one the next afternoon, Cole stood outside an office with a "manager" sign taped to the door. So far, he had no uniform except for his glove and shoes. At precisely one o'clock, Whitsel opened his office door and said, "Welcome, Cole. I'm glad you're here. I'll not fool you, we're in a tight place. Less than six weeks to play, and we're four games behind the Mets in St. Lucie and six games behind the Tarpons at Tampa. Four of our best players have been called up to AA at Springfield, and two of our pitchers have moved all the way up to Memphis. Seems like we're all stretched a little, but we have to do the best we can with what we've got.

"For the moment, Clint Simpson is still here. Might be the best young catcher in the league. Rumor has it, the big club in St. Louis has their eyes on him. He'll be able to help you tonight. Go get dressed. Your uniform is in the locker with your name on it. If you could get us through five or six innings, that would be a great help. Nearly all the team is already here playing cards or watching television. They know who you are, but go ahead and introduce yourself."

In the clubhouse, most players were playing cards or writing letters. Cole was fascinated with the rumor that Simpson might be in St. Louis by next year and was eager to meet him. When he found Simpson in the training room, Cole tried to introduce himself.

Before he could speak, Simpson jumped up and thumped him on the back. "Probably going to use you in a mid-relief or closer. When we warm up before the game, I plan to watch you. Hard for me to catch you if I haven't seen you pitch. See you in an hour or so."

A relief pitcher and a closer! It was the first time Cole had heard those words. *I thought I was a starter! Never heard a word about being a reliever. Guess it will be okay as long as I get a chance to pitch, as long as I get in the game.*

A few minutes before the game started, Cole threw a few pitches to Simpson while two of the coaches watched. When they finished, one coach said, "Okay, Memphis, sit in the bullpen with the other pitchers."

Cole settled down and prepared to watch. At the end of six innings, the Palm Beach Cardinals were holding on to a slim one-run lead when

Cole got the call. "Okay, Memphis, it's your game. Hold them for three innings, and we go out a winner."

Forty minutes later, the game was over. Cole had not allowed a hit, striking out six of the nine batters he faced. The Cardinals had won, and he had been a part of it. No longer a rookie, now he was part of the team. In reality, they were all rookies; some were moving up toward stardom, while others were moving down, but for the moment they were all moving forward with a common goal: to catch the Phillies and the Reds. It was not to be. Though they caught the Reds, the Phillies were too far ahead with too little time. Cole pitched every third day, and he pitched well. Several times, he noticed men watching him, and on two occasions, individuals from St. Louis were in the stands.

In the week before the season ended, Cole received a letter with a return address of M. Someday, Boston, Massachusetts. Cole had been planning to visit Tracey and hoped to renew their romance. Holding his breath, he began reading:

How's my baseball player? I hope this does not upset you, but I've been asked to be the lead doctor in a new children's hospital in Lima, Peru. My period of service is for eighteen months. It is a combination of medical and missionary work, and I feel called to do it. Do not forget me! In the short time I knew you, I became very attached to you; however, I feel God has called me to this work. By the time your season is over, I will be in Peru. When I return, I expect you will be in St. Louis. Wait for me!

I love you.

Someday.

When the season ended, Cole had planned to head toward Boston and see what developed with "Someday." Peru! *The end of the world.* Not that he was ready to get married, but he wasn't expecting *this.*

Four hours later, he was dressing for the game when one of the coaches came by and said, "Skipper wants to see you in his office."

Now what? What else could go wrong in one afternoon? Surely, they aren't going to send me back to A ball, or even worse, turn me loose.

These thoughts were interrupted when the manager came back and entered his office. "Sit down. Sit down. Adams, have a rest. You've been a big help to us. Just wish you could have gotten here earlier. Might have won the division instead of finishing three games back. Anyway, tomorrow is the last day of your contract. If you choose to go to Mexico and play winter ball, you can certainly do so, your choice, up to you. However, you have not gone unnoticed. Twice, people from the big club in St. Louis have been here to watch you.

"They would prefer you rest your arm—go home and throw with a friend every three days or so. We are prepared to offer you a new contract that would pretty much double your salary. You would come back here in the spring, and your progress after that is up to you. How would that suit you?"

"Well, to tell the truth, I've had a bad day. Got a letter I wasn't expecting from a lady friend. I accept, however. What you just told me turned my day around."

"Okay, I'll have your new contract ready for you in the morning. One other thing, you are expected to report for spring training in Jupiter, Florida, between the twentieth and the twenty-fifth of February. For the most part, we have our own field and training facility. So does AAA and so does the big club, but no doubt you'll get to pitch against some major league hitters, so get ready."

Now that there was no reason to go to Boston, Cole started driving toward Memphis. He looked forward to seeing his family and friends. But beyond that, he could not imagine sitting at home. For a week, he looked for his old friends—few of them could be found. Britches was home from his summer with the Detroit Tigers organization. They worked out together in the afternoons, but with little else to do, Cole drifted around the house. This continued until the phone rang one morning. His mother answered the phone. Laughing, she said, "Oh, he's right here," and handed Cole the phone. "It's your dad."

"Morning, Cole! What are you up to?"

"Not much. I was just looking through some travel folders, playing with the idea of going to Lima, Peru, to see a friend of mine."

"Lima, Peru? Gosh, that's halfway around the world! Come by the office about ten. I've got an idea to try out on you. I'll buy you a cup of coffee."

With a touch of curiosity, Cole got dressed and headed to the downtown Presbyterian church to see his father. When Cole entered his father's office, there was a cup of coffee and a pastry waiting for him.

"What's up, Dad?"

"Well, here's my idea. You're going to be here for about five months. You're a college graduate and a very fine professional athlete. It would be wrong for you to just sit around with nothing to do, and I have a solution. I am in a tight spot. Don Williams, my main helper, fell off a ladder at his house yesterday, broke an ankle and three ribs. I have no idea when he might be back. And the janitor has the flu. Until I can right the ship, I need your help."

"Whoa, Dad! You caught me a little by surprise there. Like I said, I had planned to go visit a lady friend in Peru. Can I let you know?"

"No, I'm sorry, but I need to do something quickly. If you can't help, I'll have to hire a temporary. There is so much to do I could use two people. Britches is home for the winter. If the two of you work for the church, you could be off by three every day, which would give you time to work out at the gym. I saw Britches yesterday, and he said, 'I will if he will.'"

Seeing he was caught in a trap, Cole could do little more than promise an answer by the next day. Escaping the church, he went to find Britches. To his surprise, Britches was inclined to accept the job.

"It'd be sort of cool. I like the idea. I've been home for a week, and I'm bored already. Besides, we could go to the gym in the afternoons, work out, and I could let you pitch to me. Any money we make, we could give it to some charity, like the Boy Scouts. Neither one of us needs money," Britches said. "I'm okay with it. I want to work with your dad. Who knows how long this job of professional baseball will last?"

Seeing he was trapped, Cole had little to say other than, "Okay, let's do it."

The next morning, they received a list of their duties.

"Let's rotate," Britches said. "Cole, you take everything outside for the first week, and I'll take the inside. In a week, we swap."

With this arrangement in place, Cole went outside to sweep the walkways, cut the grass, and trim the hedges. Britches stayed inside, making coffee for the ladies' Wednesday Bible study, sorting the mail, and answering the phone. Most days, they finished by three and headed for the gym. Three days a week, Cole pitched to Britches.

"Seems to me your fastball has more spin on it and breaking down. Really no comparison to a year ago," Britches said.

Before long, spectators started gathering to watch Cole pitch. Finally, one of the boys nerved up and asked Cole, "Do you pitch for the St. Louis Cardinals?"

Laughing, Cole responded, "No, but I might someday. My friend who is catching me plays for the Detroit Tigers."

"If I bring you a baseball, will you sign it for my little brother, Gerald?" the boy asked. "He's been pretty sick, and he's in the hospital."

"Tell you what. We have an extra ball or two. We'll sign one for him, and you tell us if your little brother gets better." Big brother was always at the gym, but Gerald remained in the hospital.

Finally, one afternoon after working out, Cole said, "Let's go to the hospital and see if we can help."

Finding the boy in the children's wing was easy, but seeing him was painful. Gerald was so skinny his ribs were visible, and it was obvious he was very sick. Getting next to his bed, Cole whispered, "Gerald, if you hurry up and get well, you can come practice with us. I'll show you how to throw a curveball, and Britches can show you how big-league hitters do."

Gerald quickly improved. Four weeks later, he waited for Cole at the gym, dressed in his Little League uniform. For the next three months, the boy was always there.

"Gerald, if I ever get to the big leagues, I'll have the whole team autograph the ball for you," Cole said.

Britches added, "If I ever hit a home run for the Tigers, I'll get an autographed bat for you."

Five months later, as Cole began his drive from frost-covered

Memphis to Jupiter, Florida, his thoughts drifted back to his little friend. Though Gerald's hands were small, he was beginning to throw a curveball with a little spin on it. Working with him was an unexpected pleasure, but working with Britches and his father had gone far better than Cole had expected. To keep from getting drowsy, he began to list some of the things he had done. At first, he had mowed the lawn and swept the leaves off the front steps. Later, he shoveled snow. He handled small tasks like answering the phone, unlocking the church in the morning, going for the mail, and making coffee. Once he taught Sunday school when the regular teacher had the flu. He went with his father to call on shut-ins, worked with the church Scout troop, and even made speeches to the local Rotary and Lions clubs about life as a professional baseball player.

Time passed quickly once Cole arrived in Florida. At first, the Cardinals' spring training complex in Jupiter reminded him of a circus. Players from the major league team in St. Louis as well as St. Louis's minor league affiliates were all in a group talking and telling stories about the past five months. By the end of the week, the teams had settled down in their own training camps. At first, the Palm Beach players kept to themselves, but by the second week, they began to play games with other minor-league teams. One afternoon, they played against a Detroit Tigers team, and Cole and Britches had a chance to visit. Cole noticed when he pitched, usually every third or fourth day, people watched him. His biggest challenge came at the end of the second week when he pitched for four innings against the Chicago Cubs major-league team, allowing only one hit.

Perhaps the highlight of spring training came a week before the end. Manager Whitsel sent a message for Cole to come by his office.

"Cole, you've had a good spring. Stayed focused with good movement on your pitches and also good control. Now, I've got a reward for you. This afternoon, you're going to be our starting pitcher against our big-league team. Pitch six innings if you can," Whitsel said, then dropped him a challenge. "Oh, and by the way, Lopez, their smart-mouth shortstop, says they're going to send you back to rookie ball."

"We'll see about that," Cole declared. "We'll just see."

When the game started, the big-league Cardinals batted first, and Lopez was the first batter. Clint Simpson, the Palm Beach catcher, came out to talk to Cole.

"To get Lopez out, you've got to keep him off the plate. Keep the pitches tight on him. Hit him if you've got to."

Following Simpson's advice, Cole pitched Lopez inside. Four pitches later, Lopez struck out and Cole was on a roll. Palm Beach scored three runs in the second. Cole only allowed two singles and struck out six batters in the six innings he pitched. Lopez struck out both times he was at bat. Palm Beach beat the Cardinals, 3–2.

While the team celebrated beating the big-league club, one of the coaches nudged Cole and said, "Get ready. Here comes trouble."

Before Cole could move, Lopez was standing in front of him. "Hey, Adams. Where in hell did you get that crazy delivery? I can't see your arm. I can't see the ball. How can I hit what I can't see? Hurry up and come to St. Louis; we got to have you there."

After he left, Cole said, "Wow! Wasn't expecting that. I thought we were about to have a fight."

"Me, too," chimed in Thompson, the second baseman.

As spring training wound down, the teams prepared to head north for the season opening. Memphis was the first to go, followed by St. Louis, while Cole and his team headed to nearby Palm Beach. The season started well. Cole pitched the first game on Opening Day, allowing only two hits and no runs in six innings. By the end of May, Palm Beach was in first place, and Cole's record was four wins and no losses.

On June 1, a day after he had pitched, Cole was sitting by his locker when one of the coaches came looking for him. "Hey, Adams! Skipper wants to see you in his office. Now!"

"What does he want with me? Have I done something wrong?"

"I have no idea. He just wants to see you."

When Cole stepped into Whitsel's office, he was surprised to find the pitching coach there as well.

"Really good game there, Cole," the coach said. "You've gotten us off to a great start. Now the bad news. We're sending you home."

Taken completely by surprise, Cole could only stutter, "What's the matter? What have I done wrong?"

Whitsel laughed.

"Why, you haven't done anything wrong! Wish we could keep you!" he said. "But you're heading up the ladder to the AAA Memphis Redbirds. We expected to lose you sometime this year, but not so soon. Morrison, the left-handed closer for St. Louis, has come down with a sore arm. Andrews, in Memphis, is moving up to replace him, and you're going to fill the hole in Memphis. Ought to be good for you; when the team is in Memphis, you can live at home. Maybe lots of your old friends and neighbors will come to watch you pitch. We're going to miss you, Cole."

Somewhat at a loss for words, he could only reply, "Thanks, Skip. I'll miss you guys, too."

Two days later, Cole moved back home, to the delight of his parents. The Memphis Redbirds manager, Hawkins, did not seem quite as excited. "Glad to have you. To be honest with you, though, Andrews is going to be hard for you to replace. Best pitcher here in Memphis in years. But again, glad you're here. You'll get your locker and uniform. Day game tomorrow; be here by nine. I expect we'll need you to pitch."

As soon as he could, Cole called Luther and Pearly to tell them he had been called up to Memphis and would likely be pitching tomorrow.

"Luther's already got the news," Pearly said. "He's downtown right now seeing if he can get box seats for tomorrow's game behind the Redbirds' dugout. I'll be there, too, along with your mama and daddy."

The Redbirds were popular in Memphis. The stadium was nearly sold out by game time the next day, and as promised, Luther and Pearly, along with Cole's parents, were seated right behind the Redbirds' dugout. It was not until the seventh inning that Cole got to pitch. In short order, he struck out the first two batters he faced, and the third flied out. The visiting Birmingham team did no better in the eighth or ninth, and the Redbirds were winners. Cole had struck out five of the nine batters he faced and had not allowed a hit. Between innings, Cole could hear Luther telling someone, "Better watch him now; he ain't gonna be here long."

In later years, Cole would remember his time at Memphis as the best of his career. By late July 1999, he was unhittable.

Then came another one of life's curveballs.

It was just Cole's second year in professional baseball and he was only one step away from St. Louis—the big leagues. Baseball was all he could think about at the time. *Could I throw a fastball at ninety-five miles per hour, or maybe a hundred? How sharp is my curveball or my slider?*

He sat in the dugout watching during the hot afternoon game—not his day to pitch—when a batter hit a foul ball past him and into the stands. When Cole looked around, there was a lady with a little boy, about nine or ten. It looked like the ball had hit the little fellow, who was holding his arm and trying not to cry. Even worse, an older boy behind them got the ball. When the game ended, Cole went after the pair to make sure the boy wasn't hurt. He found out the lady was his nurse, not his mother, and the child was a cancer patient at a nearby children's hospital—St. Jude.

Cole remembered that day so well. Months later, he called Britches to fill him in about the moment that had changed his life.

"Don't think I really looked at the nurse at first, but oh, my goodness—smokin' good-looking—well, to be honest, she made me take more interest in the little boy, John. As soon as the game was over, I went up to give him an autographed baseball and a signed baseball card. I can still remember the look on his face," Cole recalled. "Turns out the little fellow was sick. I saw him two or three times after that, and I visited him at the hospital. He was fighting it hard, and things didn't look so good. Every time I saw him, that pretty nurse, Diane, was with him. Seven or eight times I asked her out, always the same, very polite, always the same response. Said she had a boyfriend."

"So how did you finally get together?" Britches asked.

"One day she said, 'You still looking for a dinner partner?' I said no, I wasn't. She kept pushing that she knew someone who would like to go out with me. I finally agreed to a lunch date, out of curiosity. When I got to the restaurant, there was Diane."

Cole looked back fondly on that lunch with Diane.

"Hey, what are you doing here?" he asked.

"I was in the neighborhood, thought you might need company," she replied.

"What about my blind date?"

"Just a joke," she laughed. "Will I do?"

Cole responded, "You're beautiful."

Laughing, Diane took his arm and said, "Come on. Let's eat lunch."

Cole thought it was the most wonderful joke anyone ever played on him. But what a lunch it turned out to be! Suddenly he felt awkward and couldn't do anything. The first thing he did was step on her foot. When they sat down, even before they ordered, he turned over a glass of water. She thought it was funny. Lunch had just arrived when Cole's cell phone rang, startling him. He'd just started carrying the newfangled thing and was still getting used to getting calls anywhere, anytime. Even on a date.

"No way am I answering the phone," he told Diane. It finally quit ringing, but then it rang again. "Let me just see who keeps calling."

Glancing at the number, Cole saw it was a teammate. Knowing it was something trivial, he ignored it. To his surprise, the phone began ringing a third time. "Let me get this taken care of."

"Hey, Woody. Let me eat lunch, okay? I'll call you back when we're through."

Cole hung up, and the phone rang again. He answered, slightly frustrated. "What is it? Why do you keep calling?"

"They are sending a driver for you in half an hour. You need to come get your stuff. You're heading up to the bigs."

Trying to calm down, Cole hung up and stuttered, "I've got to go. I've been called up. I'm heading to St. Louis. I'm so sorry. Here's money for lunch. I'm so sorry. I'm so excited. Can I see you again when I come back?"

Diane laughed, excited for him, and stood up as he did to say goodbye.

"Go, go, go, you don't have much time. Congratulations! Call me, and one more thing." She put her arms around him and kissed him. "Now, go. Hurry, hurry, hurry."

Thirty minutes later, Cole was in the back of a limo heading for St. Louis.

"Yep, St. Louis keeps me busy," the driver said. "Take you there, bring you back to Memphis when they're through with you."

Months later, catching up with Britches, Cole chuckled about how excited and nervous he'd been when St. Louis called him up.

"I was sitting in the backseat of the limo and dozed off," Cole told his old friend. "Just as I was going to sleep, I thought, 'Greatest day of my life, called up to be a Cardinal and kissed by Diane. Can't wait to get to St. Louis, and yet, I can't wait to get back to Memphis.'"

Life is all about curveballs, Britches reminded him. Nothing in life had changed his mind or Cole's.

***

When they reached St. Louis, the driver dropped Cole off at the stadium by a door marked "Player's Entrance." Apparently, the driver and the guard at the gate were old friends, and the guard opened the gate for him without question.

A few players were on the field warming up, but most were in the clubhouse. Several had played with Cole in Memphis and immediately began harassing him. "Hey, rookie, get your tail in here. What did they do, call up somebody to pitch batting practice? We must be worse than we thought if you've come to help."

During the teasing and the welcome, Cole spotted a locker with a Cardinal uniform hanging on the door—not just any Cardinal uniform but one with his name stitched across the back. It was a sight he never forgot. As he finished dressing, the clubhouse attendant came by and said, "Skip wants to see you in his office."

When he entered, Johnson, the manager, thumped him on the back and said, "Nice to see you again. I remember watching you at spring training. You stood out. Lots of people were watching you. The feeling was a year in Memphis would be good for you, maybe come up in the fall. That was the plan, but it didn't work out like we figured. Three of our players are down right now, one for the season and the other two are day by day. I really do not expect to use you, but you never can tell. We head west to San Francisco and Los Angeles next week. I expect you will be heading back to Memphis by then, but for the moment, welcome to St. Louis. Go warm up and enjoy your stay."

Out on the field, Cole joined several other pitchers doing stretches and wind sprints. A few players strolled by, asking him about certain players on the Memphis team. When he walked back to the dugout, fans were crowded along the railing hoping for an autograph. For the next thirty minutes, he signed cards and hats.

When it was time for the game to start, Cole sat in the bullpen with the other pitchers. With little expectation of getting in the game, he chewed gum and thought about Diane back in Memphis. Actually, if the Cardinals sent him back to Memphis, it wouldn't be such a bad thing. He had made it to the big leagues. He was on the St. Louis Cardinals' roster, even if he never played in a game.

Late in the ninth inning, a call came down to the bullpen for Cole to warm up. Trying to control his feelings, he began pitching in the bullpen. A moment later, the Cincinnati batter hit into a double play, and the game was over. Game Two of the series was similar. Again, late in the game, Cole got a call to warm up, but he did not get called to pitch. Game Three was an afternoon game. After that game, St. Louis would be heading for the West Coast.

About an hour before the game, Cole got a message that the manager wanted to see him. Knowing what was coming, he stepped into the manager's office. "Got to send you back to Memphis. Robins is coming back off the disabled list, and I have to make room for him. You'll be brought up here again soon as we have need for you. Keep your uniform if you want. It makes a nice souvenir. Stay ready this afternoon, might get a chance to use you." Cole had known it was coming. He knew he had done nothing wrong, but he wished he was headed to the West Coast with the team.

Game Three was different, with the Cardinals leading 9–8. Three times the call had come to the bullpen for a new pitcher, but Cole's number was not called until the ninth inning. The bases were loaded with only one out when he got the signal to come in. Stepping carefully over the foul line for good luck, he walked to the mound.

Cooper, the Cardinals catcher, was waiting for him. "Throw to my mitt, and don't worry about anything else. This is the heart of their lineup. Keep them off balance and remember that home plate belongs to you, not them. Richards is up first, and I bet he takes the first pitch. Keep him backed off the plate. Okay, rookie? Here we go. Give 'em hell."

As Richards walked to the plate, Cole's inner voice said, "This is what you've waited for. How would Luther want you to pitch?" Knowing the answer, Cole threw a slider that pushed the batter off the plate. Just as he stepped back, the ball broke down and across the plate for a called strike. Cooper threw the ball back to the Cardinals' dugout as a souvenir of Cole's first pitch in the major leagues. Richard swung at the next two pitches, hitting neither. Cole had struck out his first major-league batter. The next batter flied out to left field, and the game was over. Cole had been on the field for less than ten minutes.

On the way to the dugout, the catcher slapped him on the back. "Been a couple of years since I caught you in Palm Beach. Seems like you're throwing harder than you used to—a lot harder. Do you have any idea how fast you were throwing?"

"No, I was more concerned with location than speed."

"Well, the speed gun measured you at 103 on several pitches. If I catch you again, I might get a new glove. Good luck to you. Hope we get to work together again."

As soon as the players showered and changed into street clothes, they began loading into buses that would take them to the airport. In many ways, Cole wished he could go with them. On the other hand, he hoped someone might be waiting for him at home. *Bet I'm the first player in the history of baseball to be excited about going back to the minor leagues.*

Cole heard a familiar voice behind him. "Got the car running and ready to go. You about ready to head to Memphis?"

It was almost ten o'clock when Cole returned home. To his surprise, his parents and Cecile were waiting for him.

"I didn't expect you had gone to the West Coast with the team and thought you just might be coming home, so we waited up for you," his mother said.

"In that case, give me a minute," Cole said. "I've got something to show you."

Stepping into another room, Cole put on his Cardinals uniform.

"How do I look now?" he asked when he walked out.

"If I had a uniform like that, I suspect I would sleep in it," said his father.

When Cole looked at his mother, her face was red, and she blinked away tears. When Cole put his arm around her, she said, "I'm so proud. So proud of you. Never thought a uniform would look so good."

"Let's see. Let's just see if I don't get to wear the Cardinal uniform again sometime soon."

The next day, Cole called Diane and said, "Hey, I'm home. I'm a lonely ballplayer. Just got into town, and I'm looking for a lunch date tomorrow. Could that be possible?"

"Only if you promise not to get any phone calls while we're eating," she replied.

"I promise. Same place? Same time?"

"Yes, but I do have a problem. Tomorrow is my day to work with John Franklin," she said. John was the little boy he'd met at the ballpark and visited at the hospital. "Could I bring him with me?"

"Yes, by all means," Cole said. "I have something for him, and I can bring it with me. And . . . I thought about you the whole time I was in St. Louis."

"Yes," she said. "I've been thinking about you, too. See you tomorrow."

The autographed baseball that Cole gave John Franklin turned out to be the biggest hit of the day. Later, Diane told Cole, "You don't know this, but John Franklin is the reason I agreed to have lunch with you. He asked about you every day, and when at first I declined your offer, he told me I was making a mistake. He was right. But the best news of all, for whatever reason, his cancer has shown significant improvement—must be something magical about baseball."

Two weeks later, as the season moved toward a close, Cole was called to St. Louis again along with three of his teammates. On the day before the season ended, Cole was called into the manager's office.

"Next year, you've got a real good shot of making it on our roster here in St. Louis," the manager said. "Rest your arm over the winter, and I look forward to seeing you in Florida in late February."

Returning to Memphis, Cole once again went to work for the Presbyterian church. Three or four days a week, he worked out at the gymnasium with Britches. Cole kept the same routine as the year before, except this time, Diane was the center of his life. On Christmas Eve, he proposed, and on Christmas Day, she agreed to become his wife.

They were married in February. Cole's father and brothers helped conduct the wedding, and John Franklin was the ring bearer. Knowing that spring training was to begin in less than three weeks, they decided to forgo a honeymoon, and Diane would accompany Cole to Florida.

When spring training began, the Cardinals watched Cole closely. His arm felt strong, and his early training exercises went well. His first pitching assignment was against a group of Cardinal rookies. In many ways, Cole felt sorry for them, knowing how hard they were trying to make the team, and yet if they did well against him, his chances of making the team would be at risk. He pitched three innings against the Cardinal rookies, and two days later, he pitched four innings against the Cleveland Indians. He did not allow a hit on either occasion.

A week later, he was scheduled to pitch four innings against the world champion New York Yankees. The Cardinals' pitching coach told him, "Bear down, Cole. This is their A team, the team that won the World Series the last two years."

Cole knew the Cardinals' management would be watching him. This was judgment day. If he did well, he would make the team. There was no need to even think about what would happen if he did not, and yet, Cole knew the Yankees wouldn't be able to hit his pitches.

And they could not. In four innings, Cole struck out six of the twelve batters he faced. Only one batter reached first base on a scratch single.

After the game, Josh Palmer, the All-Star Yankees catcher, told him, "Great job, Cole. Wish you were on our team." It would be almost eight years before they would meet again!

As spring training ended, Cole did not go back to Memphis; he went to St. Louis instead. Life in St. Louis was even better than he and Diane had imagined. They bought a small house in the suburbs, only fifteen minutes from the ballpark and ten minutes from the hospital where Diane worked. Their salaries were more than sufficient. Cole pitched far better than the Cardinals anticipated. On a number of occasions, Cole's pitching was unhittable.

Whenever Cole was mentioned in the *St. Louis Post-Dispatch*, Diane would cut out the article and mail it to John Franklin in Memphis. The little boy was in much better health, and his cancer was in remission.

Over Christmas, Diane and Cole returned to Memphis to spend the holidays with family and friends. On one afternoon, they took Mrs. Wilson and her children for a riverboat ride on the Mississippi River. The twins, James and Sarah, were grown now. James had moved into a place of his own and was working at the railroad, where Luther had gotten him a job. Sarah was in college. Baby Chrissy, who used to pull Cole's tomato plants out by the roots, was now a sweet-natured teenager and the family's main gardener. They'd turned their veggie stand into a little shop and expanded it over the years to include specialty jams, sauces, preserves, and local arts and crafts.

Another day, Cole and Diane took little John Franklin to the Memphis Zoo. They barely recognized him when they met his parents to pick him up. The boy had filled out well since his treatment finished. He looked fit and healthy. Diane's love for children was obvious, and Cole began to anticipate parenthood might not be too far away.

Two months later, when spring training began, the atmosphere was different. Cole was a regular on the team, and he no longer had to earn a spot. As the season began, he felt secure in his role as a Cardinal closer, a pitcher who could be relied on to keep the other team from scoring late in the game.

It had been a wonderful Sunday afternoon, with the Cardinals beating the Cubs for the third straight day. Cole had pitched for four innings, allowing only two hits. Tonight was the night to celebrate, and four of the players and their wives had gathered at a favorite restaurant on the Hill for an Italian dinner. As the pasta and red wine flowed, Cole noticed Diane barely picked at her food.

"Everything okay? You haven't touched your food," he asked quietly.

"I'm fine, just ate some junk at the ballpark. Sort of spoiled my appetite," Diane replied.

"Eat what you can; we'll talk when we get home."

Later, when they were at home, Cole brought it up again. "So how much weight have you lost?"

"Five or six pounds," Diane said. "We are short two nurses in the operating room. I've been on my feet for the past two weeks, no breaks or time off for lunch. Quit worrying about it. I've got my annual exam coming up anyway. I think we should start thinking about having a family. It's time to quit worrying about losing weight and start gaining weight."

Two weeks later, Diane went for her annual physical. The doctor, like Cole, seemed concerned about her loss of appetite and decline in weight. Though Diane seemed more tired than usual, she attributed this to her heavy workload. After a routine exam, the doctor ordered some blood work and told her, "I'm sure everything will be fine."

Five days later, it was just past midnight when Cole arrived home from a game against Cincinnati. He had hoped to see Diane in the seats reserved for players' wives, but she was not there and must have worked late. Tiptoeing in, he expected to find her in bed asleep. Instead, he found Diane sitting on the sofa, wrapped in a blanket.

"Honey, what—"

"We need to talk," she interrupted. "Doctor Randall called me, and he's concerned about the test results. He wants me to come back for a CT scan on Thursday. He just said that with my weight loss and abnormality in the blood work, he needs to do more tests. He said no need to panic."

Diane paused, clearly troubled, then told him, "Honey, we need to see where we are before we move toward having a family."

For a moment, there was little to do but hold on to each other. Each had their own thoughts; each had their own fears. Finally, Cole managed to say, "We'll get through this. You know we will. We always do."

Yet words didn't help, and all they could do was wait seventy-two hours and return to the doctor's office.

After the CT scan came more days of waiting and fear. It was Monday before Dr. Randall called with the report they had hoped not to hear.

"I am concerned about the image from the scan, and I want to schedule a biopsy before we go any further," he said. "I suggest we move ahead quickly with this. I have scheduled you for Thursday morning at eight."

In the meantime, the Cardinals were scheduled to be on the road for ten days, starting with games in Los Angeles and San Francisco. Prior to their departure, Cole met with the Cardinals' management to explain the situation and request to be put on a family emergency leave for ten days. The request was immediately granted.

"We'll miss you. Can't replace you," the manager said. "We'll probably call one of the Memphis players up. What we're doing right now is critical if we're going to make the playoffs. But we can handle this. We'll be okay, but what you're facing is far more important. All of our players are with you."

The biopsy confirmed what they feared. Diane had ovarian cancer. Having children could not happen. Perhaps for the first time, Diane began to realize that her life was in danger. She was a nurse; she'd guided many patients through the same terrifying, heartbreaking diagnosis and treatment regimen. She knew what came next.

Fearing the cancer had spread, she began chemotherapy in early June. Three weeks later, surgeons operated in hopes of removing or reducing the tumor. More chemo followed.

By the end of July, Diane weighed barely a hundred pounds. Cole sat by her bed every day and most of the night.

As she continued to weaken, it was obvious that she would not live much longer.

On the first of August, in a voice Cole could barely hear, Diane whispered, "Remember, we have a date for lunch. Don't forget it, and remember, you are my favorite ballplayer. I'm your best fan. I love you. I'll wait for you."

Then she was gone. Just like that, it was over. No more laughs. No more smiles. How quickly their lives together had ended.

The funeral took place in Memphis. Eleven of the Cardinals players' wives made the trip, and three generations of Diane's family came from Greenwood, Mississippi. Dozens of old friends and family members came to show support for Cole. Of all the flowers Cole received, the largest was a spray of red roses from the Cardinals.

Funeral services were held in historic Elmwood Cemetery. As a boy, Cole had loved to walk through the old cemetery, especially the area that held the mass graves from the yellow fever epidemic. Also nearby were the markers for the Union soldiers who died when the *Sultana* exploded just outside the Memphis Harbor.

Cole felt as if his body were frozen. He could talk; he could move, but he seemed to have no feeling. He was surrounded by his family. Luther and Pearly stood by him, along with Mrs. Wilson and her family. Britches had gotten permission to leave the Detroit Tigers for the funeral. The crowd was there not only to comfort Cole but to help him remember Diane. Then, one by one, they were gone, and Cole was left to remember alone.

The last thing Cole wanted was to return to St. Louis.

He was under contract, and he had agreed to pitch for the Cardinals. He did not want to do so, but he was a professional, and he would finish the season. To his surprise, putting on his uniform and returning to the team was not as bad as he imagined it might be. The Cardinals were fighting the Reds for a spot in the playoffs, and Cole found baseball a welcome distraction from his personal problems.

Two days after the end of the season, Cole received a call from the Cardinals' front office. "Good morning, Mr. Adams. Lane Stevens, our senior vice president of player personnel, would like to schedule a meeting with you to discuss your next year's contract. Would tomorrow at eleven be convenient with you?"

"Yes, that will be fine. Tell Mr. Stevens I look forward to talking to him," he replied.

Cole hung up the phone, knowing the bridge he was about to cross but not willing to talk about it yet. How easy it would be to take the money—to continue his career. He was at the top of his game, the best left-handed relief pitcher in the National League. Since he was a little boy, pitching had been his dream. Then it had been their dream. Now, Diane was gone. The dream was over. It was time to move on.

Dreading his talk with the Cardinals' top brass, Cole remembered a bottle of bourbon that had been in his car since the funeral. He brought it into the house and said, "Got to start down another road." He emptied the bourbon down the sink. Step one in the right direction.

The next morning at eleven, he was ushered into the personnel chief's office overlooking the Arch and the Mississippi River. Admiring the view, Stevens stood near a wall of large windows.

"Hard to imagine those early settlers heading west from here, leaving everything behind for new lives," Stevens said, turning to Cole with a smile. "That's sort of what you're doing, isn't it?"

"How could you possibly know what I was thinking?" Cole asked, surprised.

Stevens gestured for Cole to join him in a cozy area with couches and a view out the windows.

"Years ago I lost a child, my little boy, in a swimming pool accident. At the time, I was a professional golfer on the big tour. I never hit another golf ball. I came home to my family and never looked back," Stevens said. "Tell me what your plans are, Cole. We are prepared to more than double your salary if that's what you want, and there is a significant signing bonus."

"No, Lane. It's time for me to hang up my uniform," Cole said. "The Cardinals have been more than good to me, but it's time to move on. If they will have me, I plan to enter seminary next fall to be a preacher."

"Somehow I guessed that's where you were heading," Stevens said. "The Cardinals will miss you. There is no way to replace you. May God bless you on your journey."

***

The next few weeks would have been brutally lonely, if Cole hadn't had so much to do to prepare himself for a new life. He listed the house with a real estate agent, sold Diane's car, and gave her clothing and furniture to Goodwill. He closed her bank account, where she had substantial savings. After talking to her parents, he donated the money to St. Jude, where John Franklin and so many other children received top-notch treatment. Diane would have wanted it that way.

On the first day of November, Cole packed his car and headed toward Memphis.

Then he was home. Home where his parents lived. The home where he had grown up but not exactly his home now. More than home, it was a place to return before starting on some new path. A place to pause and rest before beginning anew.

Two nights after his return, Cole joined his father in the upstairs office. For the first time in his life, he accepted his father's offer of a cigar. After some small talk, Cole said, "What are the chances of me getting into seminary next fall?"

"So you're really going to do it? Give up baseball and be a preacher?"

"Yes, if seminary will have me, I'm ready to go. It's not something I just thought of. Diane and I talked about it before she got sick. It was a journey we were looking forward to. Now, that dream is gone for the two of us, but if she were here, she would want me to move on."

"Well, my preference would be Columbia Theological Seminary in Decatur, Georgia," Cole's father replied. "It's where I went, and both of your brothers went there. The dean is a good friend of mine, but you did well in college and should have no problem being accepted. Probably the best thing would be to call or write and ask them to send you an admission application. You might like to look at Union Theological in Richmond. Both of your brothers will be here next week, and you can see what they have to say."

A week later, during a family dinner, Cole's plan was the center of discussion. "Can you imagine four Presbyterian ministers from one family? That ought to be some sort of theological record," Cole said.

"No," his dad laughed. "I'm sure some Baptist or Methodist family can top that."

Cole's older brother Bill smiled and talked to his other brother Joseph, whispering about what Cole would have in front of him.

Cole said, "How much wine have you had?"

"None. I'm just looking forward to having you learn Greek so we can talk," Bill grinned.

"That will be an adventure. I have enough trouble speaking English."

Two months later, Cole was accepted to begin classes at Columbia Theological Seminary in July. Now that he knew when and where he was going, he had several months to get ready. For the second time in his life, he had accepted a job on the church staff at minimum wage, doing everything from mowing the lawn to teaching Sunday school. In his spare time, he read the Bible, concentrating on parts of the Old Testament that were less familiar. On Sundays, he watched his father preach. Cole wondered if he could do nearly as well.

For the first time since before Diane got sick, he felt like he was moving toward something good.

***

At long last, it was time to head toward Georgia and seminary. It was July 2002, and Cole was twenty-seven years old. To his surprise, he wasn't the oldest student. There were more than fifty people in the class. Some had just finished college, but some were older than he was. One man was in his early sixties. For the summer, they had only one professor and only one class: Greek. Years later, he could still remember the first day: "Ladies and gentlemen, welcome to Columbia Theological Seminary. You have sixty days to become comfortable with the Greek language. Some of you may not make it, but . . ."

For Cole, the sixty days of Greek were both fun and easy. One afternoon, about twenty students went into Atlanta to watch an afternoon game between the Braves and the Cardinals, his old team. Sitting in the outfield bleachers and drinking beer, the group chatted and kept score in Greek. Cole could not escape a sense of nostalgia as the Cardinals' pitching collapsed.

At the end of the summer, the class was comfortable with Greek and ready to move on. In Cole's first year, he took classes in the Old and New Testament, pastoral care, and his first practices in preaching. In his second year, he became comfortable with Hebrew and completed an internship at a healthcare center.

Now twenty-eight, Cole could have been at the peak of his baseball career. But he didn't miss baseball as much as he'd thought he might, even when he heard that his old buddy, Socrates, had signed a contract to play for the Cardinals, following the same track Cole had started years ago. It would have been something special to play on the same team with the kid who'd tagged along trying to coach Cole and Britches and copying Luther word for word.

In Cole's last year of seminary, he focused on pastoral care, prayer, and preaching at a small church. This proved to be a real success as he was able to weave in parts of his baseball career with stories from the Bible. Unlike many of his classmates, Cole was a natural storyteller, and preaching was relatively easy.

Early in the spring of his third year, Cole realized he would soon graduate with a Master of Divinity degree and had to decide what he would do next. For much of the past year, Cole had served as an interim pastor at a small church less than half an hour away from the seminary. Since it was a good experience, he hoped he might find a similar opportunity in the future.

He heard about a small church in Denmark, Georgia, that was looking for a pastor. There was something familiar about the name. Finally, he remembered that his father had served as a minister there. It was his father's first church, and Cole's brother Bill had been born in Denmark. Several weeks later, three members of the Denmark church visited the seminary to meet with some pastoral candidates. The previous pastor at Denmark Presbyterian Church was an older man who had left the church for health reasons. The church had been without a pastor for six months.

Two men and one woman interviewed Cole. The men seemed more interested in Cole's years as a professional baseball player, and one remembered seeing Cole pitch against the Atlanta Braves. The lady asked if Cole had ever visited Denmark.

"No," said Cole, "but Denmark was my father's first church."

"Oh, my goodness!" the lady responded. "We had no idea that you had that connection! Well, let me ask you this, if the church extended an offer to you, would you be interested in coming to Denmark to be our pastor?"

"Well, I am just beginning the process, so you are the first church I have talked to," Cole said. "Of course, I need some time to pray about this and talk to my family, but thank you for your interest in me."

At last, Cole graduated from seminary. He went home to spend a quiet week with his parents and sister. It gave him time to consider his next step. He had received three offers from churches that would like for him to serve as their next minister. One was from a large church that was expanding rapidly in a suburb just north of Miami, Florida. He did not have a good feeling about it.

He visited the second church, located on the Georgia coast, which had made a good offer that appealed to him. He had visited there several years ago for the beginning of the shrimp season. Cole leaned toward accepting the second church.

The third offer was from the Presbyterian church in Denmark, Georgia. It was a historic church, established long before the Civil War. It had been his father's first church and was an obvious place to start his ministry. However, the sanctuary needed repairs, there were few young families in the congregation, and the proposed salary was the lowest of the three.

He needed to make a decision soon. Cole secretly wished his father would tell him which offer to accept, but that was not to be. Over and over, he said that he had to feel which church needed him—was truly calling him—not just offering him a job. Where was God leading him?

After dinner, Cole tried to watch a baseball game but soon gave up and dressed for bed. Even though he knew many of the players, the game held little interest for him. Once he had been there and was a part of the team, but that was another time, another world. Turning off the light, he drifted into a restless sleep.

In his dreams, Cole felt the presence of something, or someone. He tried to move but could not. He tried to cry out for help but made no sound. For a second, he felt the sensation of flying. Suddenly, he was standing in front of a weathered brown church with a historic marker near the front door that read, "Denmark Historic Presbyterian Church." Then he heard a soft, gentle voice say, "Here."

He awoke covered in sweat. The bedcovers were on the floor. Not sure what, if anything, had happened to him, he drifted off into a dreamless sleep.

In the morning, Cole recounted the dream to his father, who said, "And you're still not sure where to go!"

Cole began to feel that perhaps Denmark was the place he needed to be. After two more days of thinking, worrying, and praying, Cole accepted the offer to become the preacher at the First Presbyterian Church in Denmark, Georgia.

Even though Cole had never visited Denmark, he felt comfortable following in the footsteps of his father, Reverend Dan. Two weeks later, he packed his car and began the drive to Denmark. On the second day of his trip, he realized that the town was less than an hour away. Perhaps it would be fun to see what his new church would be like on Sunday morning.

As Cole's curiosity grew, he stepped on the gas, and thirty minutes later, he passed a sign proclaiming, "Denmark: What America is meant to be!" Not sure what to expect, he drove down Main Street. There was a church on every block, but he did not see a Presbyterian church. Thinking he had overlooked it, he turned around and retraced his route. On the left, he noticed several couples entering a small brown building with a historic marker in front of it. Curious as to what it might be, he realized the building with stained glass windows looked like something he might have found in London. To the left of the entrance was a state of Georgia historic marker that read, "First Presbyterian Church of Denmark, established 1832—used by Federal Soldiers in 1863 in the Atlanta Campaign as a field hospital. Restored after the war, it has served as a Presbyterian Church for more than 150 years."

The sign on the door read, "First Presbyterian Church—Worship: 10:30, Sunday School: 9:30." Looking at his watch, Cole realized the worship service would start in fifteen minutes. He parked his car, slipped on a coat, and walked up the steps to the entrance.

Taking a program, he sat near the door. Some forty or fifty people were already seated, most looking at him. Perhaps they thought he had dropped in from a foreign country or maybe the moon. Could someone from Memphis be so different from people in Georgia? He thought it best to just smile and look at the program. A moment later, the organist began playing, the choir processed in, and he was forgotten. Since the church was without a pastor, the congregation watched a film of mission work in Peru, supported in part by the church. The room temperature was more than eighty degrees and climbing. Surely people in Georgia had air conditioning. Cole thought that next week he'd have it set at about sixty degrees to keep them awake.

At the end of the service, one of the ushers thanked everyone for being there and apologized for the broken air conditioning. Then, looking right at Cole, he said, "Do we have any guests with us today?"

Cole had to say something, so he said, "I am from Memphis, and I enjoyed being with you today."

"We don't get many folks from that part of the country. What brings you to Denmark?"

Knowing it was time to admit who he was, Cole replied, "Well, friends, my name is Cole Adams, and I have been called to be your new pastor."

For his first few days in Denmark, Cole survived on canned food and the church ladies' casseroles. By day four, he was ready for a breakout. It was time to explore the neighborhood and see what groceries were available. He remembered a sign on a nearby building that advertised "Sunshine Groceries: Fresh Biscuits Every Morning By 5 AM."

He needed a little sunshine, so he walked three blocks to the combination café and grocery store. A sign on the door proclaimed, "If you can find better food and lower prices, don't tell anybody!" Somewhat tickled by that, he walked in and ordered a ham biscuit and a large mug of coffee. Preparing to pay, he was surprised when the owner replied, "No, Preacher, the first one is on us. Welcome to Denmark. We're glad you're here."

Cole was about to sit down at the counter when a nearby voice said, "Come join us, Pastor; don't sit by yourself. Come tell us about life in the big city."

Feeling somewhat awkward, he joined a group of about ten men who introduced themselves as longtime members of the Liars' Table. Laughing, one of the group said, "We're all Methodist, but we don't bite much. Tell us about life in Memphis."

Surprised to find such a welcome, Cole was enjoying his coffee and biscuit when cheers and applause broke out near the front door. A moment later, the largest dog he had ever seen walked up to the table. "What in the world is that? A Great Dane mixed up with a retriever?"

A man across the table said, "He comes in here every morning about nine fifteen. We don't know who he belongs to or where he lives, or what he is. Every one of us has tried to take him home and make a pet out of him, but he won't do it."

Another man laughed and said, "I thought Great Danes had bottles of rum around their neck, but someone must have got his."

With great dignity, the dog walked around the table and stopped by each man until he received part of a biscuit. *Good thing he only wants a biscuit instead of my arm,* Cole thought. "Does he have a name?"

"Well," replied a heavyset man on Cole's right, "we named him Lucifer, 'cause the first time he came in, he scared the hell out of us."

When the big dog came to Cole, he stopped, stared, and then put out his right paw. "Damn," the man on Cole's left whispered. "He intends to shake hands with you."

Not sure what to do, Cole shook hands (or paws) with the dog and gave him the rest of his sandwich.

"Where does he go at night? Surely people see him."

"Not so," replied another man. "He just seems to disappear."

"What's he doing? He just keeps staring at me."

"Don't know, never seen him act like that. Sure he don't belong to you?"

The big dog continued around the table, gathering scraps and parts of sandwiches. "Now watch him," whispered one of the men. "He usually disappears when the food is gone."

This time, instead of leaving, the dog circled back around and sat down next to Cole.

"Preacher, how long you been in this town?"

More than a little embarrassed, Cole responded, "Less than a week."

"And you've never seen this dog before?"

"No, not until a few minutes ago, and I will further testify I have never had the honor of owning a dog, not even as a child. Wouldn't even really know how to take care of one. My dad is a preacher with a house full of kids. It was all he could do to keep food on the table. Not much left for dogs to eat." As the dog finished circling the table, he came back to Cole and gently sat down with his head resting on Cole's knee.

In a few minutes, the group began to break up, but each man stopped by Cole to welcome him to Denmark and comment on the dog's peculiar behavior. Lifting the dog's head off his knee, Cole whispered, "Hey, buddy, I've got to buy a few groceries and start setting up housekeeping. Good to meet you."

Walking around the little store, Cole realized that although it was small, it seemed to have as much to offer as some of the big chain groceries. He had more than he could carry, so he asked the owner to hold the items until Cole could come back with his car.

"Why no, certainly not. I'm Eddie Browning, a member of your church. We deliver, and I'll bring them by your parsonage in a few minutes," the owner said. "So glad you're here. From the looks of things, it might be a good idea for me to include a sack of dog food."

As Cole started to protest, he looked to his left and saw the dog sitting by the door waiting for him. He thanked the owner and started out the door.

"Hey, pal, you need to go home. I don't know anything about dogs, especially one as big as you," Cole told the animal. Unsure what to do, he kept walking, as did the dog. When Cole reached his house, the dog bounded up the front steps and stood waiting by the front door. With little choice, Cole opened the door, and the dog shot through into the house.

Thinking it was time to gain control of the situation, Cole tapped his foot on the floor and said, "Now, you sit!" As carefully as he could, the dog sat down and looked up at Cole with an expression that seemed to say, "Have I done something wrong?"

Knowing he was beaten, Cole said, "Okay, you win. I'll give it a try, but you go to the bathroom one time in this house and it's all over. Okay?" Luc's response was to watch him with an air that said, "I would never do anything like that."

Preparing the evening meal was easy; church ladies had sent casseroles, soups, fried chicken, cakes, and pies since Cole arrived in Denmark. After dinner, he spent several hours preparing for his first sermon. He recalled advice from his father: every sermon a pastor preaches cannot and will not be excellent, but the sermon people remember is usually the first one a new preacher makes. When Cole prepared to go to bed, just as soon as he turned the house lights off, he heard a thump from the direction of the bedroom.

"Oh no, you don't," he muttered and sprinted to the back of the house. Too late. Luc curled up in the middle of the bed. "You know this is not going to happen. Get up!" The dog's only response was to yawn. Pushing and pulling was to no avail. The dog was too large.

"What if I take my belt and whip you? We'll see who the boss is." Luc's sole response was to look at him with a sad expression. Realizing the battle was lost, Cole struggled to move the dog to the other side of the bed. "If you snore, you have to sleep in the yard. I haven't slept with anyone since my wife died."

WANDA STANFILL

As Sunday drew near, Cole knew he would have to be at his best. His new church had waited more than six months to have a pastor, so the rumor was that some of the Baptists and Catholics were coming to watch the show.

Eating a breakfast of cold cereal, Cole realized how nervous he was. He remembered pitching in Game Six in New York, with ninety thousand people screaming and pulling against him, but then he was part of a team. His Cardinals teammates were behind him, and together they won the game that day, but that was different. Today, he would be out there alone with no teammates.

Then Cole remembered a story of his father's. Dan Adams had been a new preacher, facing his first sermon with a case of nerves. Young Dan had asked a friend and mentor—a preacher with decades of sermons behind him—what he must do to succeed. The older man's advice lingered with Dan forever after.

"First you must set yourself on fire, and then people will come to watch you burn," the elderly minister had said.

Lord, help let me light a fire, Cole prayed as he dressed in his best suit and prepared for church.

After the opening organ music ended, he walked past the lectern and stood in front of the congregation. A hush fell over the room.

"Good morning, church! Some of you met me last week; some did not. My name is Cole Edward Franklin Adams. I am a native of Memphis, Tennessee—a very long way from here. My father has been a Presbyterian minister for more than thirty years. When he first began his ministry, he came to this church, which was his first church, and some of you may remember him. My oldest brother Bill is a Presbyterian minister in Louisville, Kentucky, and my brother Joseph is a Presbyterian minister near Atlanta. I have a sister, Cecile, who is an administrative assistant in my father's church in Memphis."

He paused a beat, letting that family history sink in and looking around the room, trying to invite folks into his story.

"All I ever wanted to do was play baseball. When I was twelve years old, I got in a fight with a bully and hurt my right arm. After that, I learned to use my left arm to bat and pitch. I came south on a baseball scholarship at Mississippi State University in Starkville. After I graduated, I signed a contract to pitch for the St. Louis Cardinals organization. A couple years later, while pitching for the Memphis Redbirds, I met a young nurse at St. Jude Children's Research Hospital. We were married a year later. By then, I was pitching for the St. Louis Cardinals.

"Less than two years after we got married, my beautiful Diane died of cancer. I was twenty-six, still young by many standards, but my life and my dreams changed. I retired from baseball and went to seminary to become a preacher. You are my first church, and today is my first sermon."

He paused again, looking around at pews full of friendly smiles and beaming faces.

"One last thing I will tell you about myself. A few days ago, soon after I arrived here in Denmark, I was having coffee with a group of men at Sunshine Grocery when in walked this large dog named Lucifer. He had no owner and adopted me. I have never owned a dog, and now I do. He followed me home step by step. So today you get not only a new preacher but also a new friend whose name I've shortened to Luc. Come here, Luc."

At that point, the dog walked down the aisle and sat by the preacher. "The only thing Luc does not like is for people to miss church or go to sleep while I'm preaching. Let us now turn our hearts and minds to the worship of Almighty God."

Chuckling and shuffling to see the dog, Cole's congregation settled in to hear him preach.

***

The parsonage lawn had been ignored for several months, so the next week, Cole set about cutting and trimming the grass. Under a large limb in the back yard, he found a rubber baseball. Flipping it across the yard, he said, "Fetch, Luc!" It was the first time in a while he had thrown a ball, and it surprised him how pleasant it felt.

A week later, Cole was cleaning up his office when Mrs. Patterson, the church secretary, knocked on the door. "Preacher, I hate to bother you, but there's a man out here, says you have his dog."

"Well, Luc, looks like your family has come for you. You may be heading home."

When the dog's owner walked into Cole's office, he was not what Cole expected. Short and overweight, the man had a heavy odor of alcohol about him.

"Don't know how you got the dog, don't really care. I just came to get him," he said.

As soon as the man began speaking, Luc began to growl. Moving toward the dog, the man muttered, "You damn dog, I'll teach you some manners when I get you home."

"Sort of think that won't happen," Cole said, moving to stand in front of Luc. "No, I don't believe it will. And the way that dog is acting, I don't much think he wants to go with you. I think he is pretty happy here."

"Well, that works just fine for me—don't think I've ever whipped a preacher before," the man said.

"Don't be stupid. I'm twice as big as you, much younger, and I'm not drunk. Now, tell me who this dog really belongs to."

"He belongs to my son. We live outside of town, and he got loose when we came into Denmark a few weeks back. The boy's outside with my wife and the baby."

"Let me go and talk to them. Maybe we can make a deal. You stay here in my office."

Outside in a rusty old truck, Cole found a lady holding a baby. Sitting behind her was a boy, about ten years old. Cole introduced himself and told the boy, "Apparently, I have your dog."

"I'm sorry, but I'm not sure that's a bad thing," the woman said, before her son could answer. "We barely have enough money for food, and he goes and gets that dog. He thinks you'll pay him for it, and if you give him any money, it's just going down the street to that liquor store."

The boy in the back remained quiet.

"What if I pay you? How much did he give for him?"

"Not much, twenty dollars or so. He got it from some family that didn't want it because it got too big."

"How will this do? Is this enough?" Cole asked as he gave her ten twenty-dollar bills.

Startled, the woman said, "You know this is too much, way too much."

"Preachers do strange things sometimes. Use the money for food," he said, then turned back to the boy. "Young man, you come visit Luc anytime you want."

When he returned to his office, the man was waiting for him. "Where's the money?"

"Gave it to your wife."

"Oh, how much?"

When Cole said he gave the woman two hundred dollars, the tension in the room seemed to slip away.

"You know that's too much," the man said.

"Perhaps it was. Perhaps it wasn't enough. She said you needed money for food. Preachers do things like that sometimes."

The man stood up to leave, then paused and turned around.

"Sorry for the way I acted," he said, with his head down. "I don't know myself these days. I got hurt in an accident. Out of work for two months. When I came back, the job was gone. Been riding around looking for work ever since. Not your problem. Hope you like the dog."

At a loss for words, Cole replied, "Give me a couple of weeks. I might be able to help."

Sometime later, Mrs. Patterson stopped by Cole's office. "Not my business, but was that Sam Atkins?"

"Sure was. Do you know him?"

"Not really. I thought that was him. Pretty sad story. He used to be the best carpenter and handyman in Denmark."

"Let's think about how we can help him," Cole said. "He said he would come back in two weeks. I really hate to think about them not having money to buy food."

Two weeks later, Sam Atkins came back. "Still looking, Preacher. Not many jobs out there. Not for me, anyway. I guess I got a reputation."

"Are you sober?"

"Yes, you might remember, you gave the money to my wife! But—if I had money, I wouldn't use it for that."

"I'm willing to give you a chance—a three-month trial period here at the church," Cole said. "Staying sober is part of the deal."

"When could I start?" Sam asked, feeling hopeful for the first time in months.

"Right now. The church air conditioner is out again, and the roof is leaking. See what you can do."

In later years, Cole would look back on the day he hired Sam Atkins as one of the highlights of his ministry.

Cole's custom was to go out for dinner on Sunday night. Though he was a more than adequate cook, he remembered the old expression, "Cooking's not much fun when you're home alone."

He'd had a long day, preaching and then teaching a Sunday school class for young people, followed by home visits. Usually, an Italian meal and a glass of wine helped to ease the tiredness and get him ready for the next week.

Following a long-standing tradition, Cole asked Jeremy, the waiter, "Hey, didn't I see you in church this morning?"

"You did, for sure, wouldn't miss it for the world," Jeremy answered. "You know, one day I'm going to fool you and come more regularly. Lately folks tell me you can really lay a sermon on them, but don't you be surprised, I'm coming, I really am."

"I'll be ready for you. I've got a special sermon on sinners and redemption, just for you."

"Whoa, I can barely wait," Jeremy mumbled as he moved toward the kitchen.

After Cole's dinner arrived, he watched a ballgame on the television over the bar. He didn't keep up much with baseball now; he was really too busy, but a young left-handed pitcher sent his thoughts back to years ago in Memphis.

In other towns of similar size, the end of the season for men's baseball teams would have been of little consequence. Denmark, Georgia, was different; during the summer months, eight churches fielded teams. Some smaller churches had just enough players, while the Baptists had plenty. Six church teams had already been eliminated from the playoffs, and only the Baptists and Presbyterians were left.

It was unusual for a small church, such as the Presbyterians, to challenge the Baptists. The Presbyterian team, known as the Frosties, had only ten players, but they were good ones. The pitcher was the star; a recent convert from the Methodists, he was the reason for the team's success. If he got hurt or sick, the Frosties would be in serious trouble. At first, everyone assumed that Cole would play for the Presbyterians; however, to their surprise, he did not join the team.

"I'm honored to be asked to pitch, but I need to decline," he said. "While baseball was once an important part of my life, I now have commitments to our church that I must honor, such as a capital campaign for the addition to our sanctuary. I know we only have ten players. If one of them is hurt or unable to play, I'll put on my uniform so we don't have to forfeit."

Perhaps because the Presbyterians had so few players, or perhaps because of the way they played, more people began to come out and watch them. The local newspaper referred to their appeal as David against Goliath. As the team continued to win, attendance at the Sunday morning service began to increase. Pleased with the growing congregation, Cole laughed and said, "Perhaps good baseball is better than good preaching."

As the day for the championship drew near, many ladies cooked fried chicken or baked cakes and pies for a picnic after the game. A festive crowd filled the old park with groups of people along the sidelines and behind the centerfield fence. People began cheering when the Presbyterian team took the field. The Baptist team had won the championship for the last five years, and sentiment clearly favored the underdog Presbyterians.

"Wouldn't it be great if all these people came to church on Sunday?" Cole mused, but that thought vanished when the game began. A flash of red in the stands behind first base caught Cole's eye. A lady in a bright red shirt held a sign that said, "Go Presbyterians!" It was an omen. Maybe they could win.

The action started much too quickly. The first two Baptist players walked and the third hit a single—Baptist 1, Presbyterian 0—and the game had just begun. At that point, Chris Montgomery, the Presbyterian pitcher, shook himself and then began to throw strikes. No more Baptists reached base.

The Baptist pitcher, Evans Wilson, was unhittable. A former minor-league pitcher for the Red Sox, he was the reason the Baptists had won the championship every season since the league began five years ago, and it looked like they would do it again.

Though the crowd cheered for both teams, the Presbyterians gave them little to cheer about in the first five innings. No one expected the team to keep up with the Baptists, but at the end of five innings, the score was still 1-0. The teams played only seven innings, and in the sixth inning, the Baptists got three men on base but could not bring them home. Suddenly, when the Presbyterians came to bat, the improbable happened. The first two batters reached base, but the next two struck out and Ted Moore, the first baseman, flied out to center. It had been their best chance, but nothing had come of it.

As the seventh and last inning approached, the score was still 1–0 in favor of the Baptists. Certainly the Presbyterians had done much better than anyone expected, but a loss would still be a loss.

The first batter for the Baptists hit a slow groundball between the pitcher's mound and first base. Montgomery, the Presbyterian pitcher, moved toward the ball, but his right leg caught in the dirt, and he fell, clutching his knee. It was apparent he would not continue. At first, it seemed the Presbyterians would have to forfeit. The Baptists were already beginning to pack up when they realized that someone was on the mound beginning to warm up. Excitement rippled through the crowd as they recognized the Presbyterian preacher.

Cole had been in Denmark for more than two years, but no one had seen him throw a baseball. Only one little boy knew his secret. For months, he had watched as the preacher threw baseballs at a severely battered-looking pitching target in his back yard. When Cole was frustrated at his inability to grow the church membership, he would throw until he was exhausted. On other days, happy days, when something good had occurred in the church, he threw the baseball to celebrate.

One day when the heat was nearly unbearable, Cole turned around and told the boy, "Come on, Pete, let's go inside and eat some ice cream."

"How long you been knowing I was back there?"

"Guess I always knew. When I was your age and trying to learn to pitch, my best friend used to hide in the flowers and watch me. His name was Britches Malone, nicknamed Britches because he couldn't keep his pants up. He plays outfield for the Tigers now. You can see him on TV."

As Cole started toward the field, Pete passed him, yelling, "Preacher's coming! Preacher's coming!" Cole was surprised to see the manager of the Baptist team, Mark Rustam, waiting for him on the field.

"Got a deal for you, Preacher," Rustam said. "Your team has done good, played hard, been a tough opponent, and now your pitcher is hurt. Let's call it a draw. We can keep the trophy, and we can play again next year. How does that suit you?"

"I sort of hate to disappoint the big crowd," Cole responded. "They would like to see a winner. Thank you, but no. Let's finish the game. I am on the roster, have been all season, so I will take our pitcher's place."

Cole's response seemed to irritate Rustam. "Okay, have it your way, but expect no mercy from us."

Instead of a regular warm-up, Cole threw several soft pitches to the catcher, Pat Winston, and called the infield and Winston in for a quick talk.

"We'll be okay," Cole said. "I can still pitch, but they don't know that. I'm going to throw two wild pitches just for fun, and then I'm going to bear down. Get ready."

The first pitch was so high that Winston had to jump for it. The second was behind the batter but very soft. Everyone was laughing at Cole's apparent inability to throw strikes. However, the next three pitches were like rockets, all strikes, and the batter never had a chance. The second batter was no better, and the last batter grounded it out to third base. Even though the Baptists had failed to score in the seventh, they still led 1-0. Cole was scheduled to bat fourth, so someone would have to get on base for him to bat. Riggins, the second baseman, struck out and Doug Harris, the left fielder, popped out to the shortstop.

With only one out left, many Baptist fans stood up, anticipating a victory, but the unexpected occurred. Harrison, the third baseman, was hit by a pitch and went to first base, much to the Baptists' displeasure. All the Presbyterians were standing and cheering for Cole. Jimmy Harris, the local pharmacist, was quick to point out that no one had seen Cole bat. After all, he was a pitcher, and pitchers aren't good hitters. Now they would find out.

Chatter and yells died down as Cole walked to the plate. When he was ready to bat, he looked back to the Baptist catcher and said, "If I hit a home run, will you come to the Presbyterian church one Sunday?"

"Yeah, and if you don't, you give me fifty bucks."

"Done," Cole whispered as he stepped to the plate. The first pitch was a curve for a called strike. The next pitch was a curveball for strike two. Guessing the next pitch would be a fastball, Cole whispered, "You wanna double the bet?"

"Yeah, and if you win, I'll consider changing churches."

Very few people ever forgot what happened next. As Cole predicted, the pitch was the pitcher's best fastball, designed to strike him out and end the game. It didn't happen that way. The pitch was on the outside of the plate. Cole swung, and there was a long *crack* as the bat hit the ball. At first it looked like a fly ball. The center fielder moved back toward the fence, then stopped and turned around. The ball went far beyond the diamond, farther than they could imagine. The crowd roared as Cole ran the bases. The Presbyterians had won the game 2–1 and won the championship for the first time.

Several boys ran behind the wall, hoping to find the baseball, but despite their efforts, it was never found. Some said the ball was destroyed by the impact. The kids joked that the ball had gone into orbit and was circling the earth. At any rate, it was the longest home run anyone in Denmark had ever seen, and the disappearance of the ball only added to the legend.

Minutes later, at the trophy presentation, Cole responded to questions about whether he would play with the team in the future.

"No, I'm a preacher, not a baseball player," he said. "I want to watch the team play and hopefully watch them win more championships. My job as pastor is to win championships for my Lord and Savior, Jesus Christ."

Just after Labor Day, Cole's secretary stuck her head into his office. "Sorry to bother you. I know you're busy, but there's a lady in my office who needs to see you. She said it was about a new eye clinic."

"Seems like she needs to be talking to a banker rather than a preacher, but perhaps she wants to join the church. Send her in."

When the woman came into Cole's office, she said, "Reverend Adams, nice to see you again."

"Yes," he responded. "Pardon me, but do I know you?"

Though the woman looked familiar, her large hat and sunglasses covered her face.

"Yes, Cole, but it's been a few years," she said, smiling. "I told you someday—maybe someday—you'd see me again. Someday is today!"

Cole could not speak. He was in shock.

"At last," he whispered. "Tracey—Tracey, is that you?"

"Yes, Cole, some lady you once accidentally proposed to."

Cole stood and stepped toward her for a hug, but Tracey held up a hand to stop him.

"No, Cole, let's talk. It's been ten years since you've seen me. Are you ready for me to reappear?" she asked. "I've been to your church two Sundays. You didn't see me, though your big dog once sat near me."

They had exchanged a few letters over the years, though not for some time. Cole had written to Tracey after he met Diane; he'd felt he owed her that. When his wife died, Tracey had sent a letter expressing sympathy. He'd last written to her shortly after he came to Denmark. Now, Tracey had an opportunity to open an eye clinic in Denmark, she told him. She had an option on a building.

"When I last saw you, you were a college student. Now you're a preacher. I guess what I'm wondering is, are you ready for me to come back into your life?" Tracey asked, taking off her glasses and hat. "Could 'maybe someday' be today?"

As Cole enveloped her in a hug, he whispered, "Today is someday. I love you. Welcome home."

Minutes later, Tracey said, "Think I'll go see that real estate agent and exercise the option on that old clinic. Can we meet for dinner tonight? It's your turn to pay."

In the weeks that followed, they were rarely apart.

One afternoon, almost three weeks after the end of the church-league baseball season, Cole was in his office preparing a Sunday sermon. It had been raining for three days, more like a time he remembered in Memphis than the dryness of the deep south of Georgia. A leak in the sanctuary roof constantly reminded him of the need to restore the old church, still standing after more than 170 years. Despite its growth and the success of his ministry, the church did not have the money to repair the building. Perhaps he could preach about Noah's response to continuing rain. As Cole continued with this thought, Mrs. Patterson peeked into his office. "Someone here to see you. Don't think I've ever seen him before."

When the visitor came into Cole's office, he said, "Preacher, I bet you don't remember me!"

"Sorry. I don't believe I do," Cole replied.

"Been about eight or nine years. The last time I played against you, you pitched four innings and didn't allow a hit. I played fourteen years in the major leagues. Caught a lot of pitchers, but I never saw anyone like you."

Somewhat startled, Cole responded, "You flatter me. Been a long time ago. I expect your name is Josh Palmer. You were a catcher for the Dodgers and then the Yankees. Right?"

"Right on, Preacher. That was a long time ago and about forty pounds ago when you last saw me."

"Nice to see you again, but you have to be up to something. What brings you to Denmark?"

Rather than answer the question, Palmer said, "I watched you several weeks ago when you beat the Baptists. Looks like your arm is as good as ever."

"Is it? It's been about six years since I pitched for St. Louis. No, I wouldn't think my arm could be as good as it used to be. But why do you ask?"

In response, Palmer reached into his pocket, pulled out a business card, and gave it to Cole. The business card said:

Josh Palmer
Scout and Player Development
Southeast Region
New York Yankees

Not sure where the conversation was headed, Cole asked, "So what brings you here? Are you interested in someone in this area?"

"To be frank, we're interested in Cole Adams."

"You have got to be kidding! Is this some sort of Halloween joke?" Cole laughed.

"It's not a joke. The Yankees are desperate for pitchers. We have a couple of pitchers in Triple A and one in Double A, but none of them will be ready next year. I have watched you. I dropped by Sunday for church, and after the service, I spotted you pitching at a target out back with a group of kids. The kids were blown away, and so was I. I got a call and couldn't stay to say hello then. I could be wrong about you, but I don't think so. Would you let me time you with a speed gun, just to see?"

"No, Josh. I appreciate your offer. I'm flattered that a scout from the

New York Yankees thinks I could step back in time and pitch at the major-league level once again," Cole said. "Thank you for your interest in me, but no. And now, if you will forgive me, I really need to be working on a sermon."

Standing up, Palmer said, "Thank you for your time. I'll stay in touch, but I promise not to be a problem."

Knowing he would be unable to continue working on his sermon, Cole closed his office and went home early. Calling Tracey, he was lucky to catch her between patients.

"Hey, I just had the darnedest thing happen," he said. "No, no. I'm fine, just fine, nothing like that. Could we have dinner tonight? I need to tell you this face to face. I'm willing to pay for your dinner just to see your expression when I tell you the story."

"Gotta run, but you've aroused my curiosity," Tracey said. "Let's meet at seven in the bar at Coastal. See you there, Buttercup."

Cole hung up. She only called him that when she was in a good mood, which put him in a good mood, too.

When he got home, the rain had stopped, and the sun was out. With time to spare, Cole went out in his back yard and began throwing baseballs.

Cole arrived at the restaurant before Tracey that evening and was having a glass of wine in the bar when she arrived.

"Can't believe you're drinking without me," she said. "Whatever happened to you this afternoon must have been monumental. As soon as my wine gets here, I want to hear about it."

After they were seated at a table, Cole began, "Sunday morning at church, did you notice a heavyset man sitting near the back?"

"Actually, I did. Someone I had never seen before."

"His name is Josh Palmer. He is somewhat of a legend as a baseball player. Several years ago, I was up with the Cardinals, and I played against him. He had a long career with the Yankees."

"What does this have to do with you?"

"He's a scout for the New York Yankees, and he is interested in me."

"What? To do what? To be a scout?"

"No. To be a player. Here's his business card."

"I need another glass of wine," Tracey said. "Aren't you too old to go back? I felt like baseball was for kids."

Cole had bowed out of baseball early by some standards, but he was now thirty-two—an age at which most professional players would be considering retirement, if they weren't already gone.

"You know how old I am. Going back as a player is not an option, but I am flattered that someone like the Yankees was interested in me. Besides, this would interfere with our plans to get married. Quit worrying and enjoy your dinner."

Four days later, Josh Palmer came back. "Cole, I know you're busy, so I'll make this quick. New York is pushing for you to at least take a look."

Before Cole could reply, Palmer laid out a new proposal. "First, no one will know about this. Second, we would like to have a doctor examine you. Third, we would like to see how fast you are throwing. All this will be done at a training site forty miles from here, not currently in use. Upon completion of this, regardless of the results, we will give you a check for $2,500. Think it over. You have my card, and I'll be back around the end of the week."

Then he was gone, leaving the papers on Cole's desk. At the bottom of the proposal was a note that said, "This check would not obligate you in any way."

At a loss for words, Cole left the envelope and decided to take a walk. He didn't want to do it. He had hoped he would not see Josh Palmer again. How easy would it be to go on with his life and leave baseball in the past? *Probably ought to call Tracey and see what she thinks of this development,* he thought.

It was lunchtime before she called him back. "So, he came back? Sort of thought he might. Same offer as before?"

"Well, it's a little different this time. They want to have a doctor examine me and see how fast I can throw a baseball."

"Did you tell him to go away?" she asked.

"As I said, it's a little different. If I do it, they will give me a check for $2,500. No catches. No obligations to do anything."

There was a long pause before Tracey answered. "Wow. I didn't expect that. These people are serious. The money is nice, but it starts the ball rolling, doesn't it? If they like what they see, they'll come after you."

"Perhaps so. We'll know more after the test."

"I want you to promise me that we will make this decision together based on what is best for us and best for the church."

Cole responded, "Yes, I promise. I won't do anything before you agree."

The next morning, Cole called the number Palmer had left. "I accept your offer. No strings attached, just what you said. You can let a doctor examine me, and I will make a reasonable number of pitches that you can monitor."

Palmer's answer was simple and direct. "Fine. If Thursday's all right, a limo will pick you up in front of the church at one o'clock. That good for you? And the check will be with the limo."

"One thing, Josh, that's fine, but my lady friend will be with me."

As soon as he hung up, Cole called Tracey to tell her the plans. "I'll make sure I don't have any appointments then," she said.

On Thursday, at precisely one o'clock, a gray limousine pulled up at the side entrance to the church. When Tracey and Cole stepped toward the car, a pleasant-looking, uniformed driver opened the rear door, touched his finger to his cap, and said, "Welcome aboard. This envelope is for the gentleman, and this orchid is for the lady. Hop in and get comfortable; we've got about a thirty-minute drive."

"How nice," Tracey whispered. "These people are really after you."

Half an hour later, they stopped in front of what appeared to be a college training facility with attached offices. Palmer was waiting with three men, including one who wore a stethoscope. Palmer introduced everyone and then said, "Cole, Dr. Watson is going to examine you. Ma'am, do you want to wait in the office or out on the field?"

"No," Tracey replied. "I'm a doctor. I'll go with him."

Forty minutes later, the exam was finished. "You are in fine shape. How much do you exercise?" the doctor asked.

Cole responded, "I run three or four days a week, and I throw a baseball every day but Sunday."

"Well, your exercise shows. You are in better shape than any pitcher I have ever examined."

"Do you have your own practice?" Tracey asked.

"No, I am an employee of the New York Yankees. Now, Cole, if you want to put your baseball shoes on, they're waiting on you."

To Cole's surprise, Josh Palmer was waiting on him with a catcher's mitt on his hand.

"Be like old times, Cole," Palmer said. "Just relax and pretend you're pitching in the National League, and I'm your catcher."

A second man with a speed gun was standing behind Josh. After a couple of warm-up throws, Cole began to throw hard. Five minutes later, Cole shouted, "Now the curve, then the slider."

After a few minutes, Palmer yelled, "Now pretend it's the World Series and there's only one batter left to win. Give it your best."

Five pitches later, Palmer held up his hand to stop. "That's enough! I swear you're throwing harder than you did when you were in the All-Star Game." Palmer looked at the tape for a minute or so.

"Don't know how hard you threw when you played for St. Louis, so it's hard to compare with today," he said.

"Well, what was it today?" Cole asked. "Felt pretty good to me."

Palmer said, "I don't think you were throwing this hard before. We clocked you at 98 or 100 miles per hour or so, and on the last pitch, it actually registered at 104!"

"How good is that machine? I thought I was throwing around 70."

"Don't think so," Palmer laughed. "Look at my hand—think I've got blisters on it."

On the way back, the limo driver said, "Nothing wrong with that machine! No, sir! No, it wasn't. I've been around, worked for these folks a long time. Played ball myself, played in the Yankees farm system and played with Josh Palmer—know him pretty good. Never seen him work so hard to catch somebody. No, sir, you're something special. Easy to see why the Yankees are after you."

At dinner that night, Tracey said, "I've been thinking about baseball. Maybe that is what you were meant to be. Like the limo driver said, you are something special. If you get a good offer, I am for it. Now, can we have another glass of wine?"

When the wine came, she said, "Do you remember our first date? That cute old man thought you proposed to me. I wish you would propose to me again."

"Funny how that started the magic between us. I hope it never ends," Cole said. Before Tracey could reply, he dropped to one knee, a gold ring with a single diamond in his hand. "Tracey, will you marry me?"

"Yes! Yes, I will!" Tracey exclaimed. "The ring is lovely! Put it on my finger quickly! How long have you had it? Where did it come from? I wish we had done this ten years ago! Yes, yes, I will be your wife! Oh, my goodness, look around us!"

People in the restaurant were standing with wine glasses raised as cheers and toasts rang out. She recognized several of their friends.

"How did this happen?" Tracey asked. "They must have known. You had this arranged!"

Cole said, "Yes, yes, I did. Don't know what I would have done if you said no."

"Don't you worry, that was never going to happen," she said.

After several rounds of toasts and congratulations, the evening finally ended. On the way home, Tracey whispered, "Biggest day of my life: all of this and the New York Yankees. Too much to think about. Soon I won't be just Dr. Livingston, but Mrs. Cole Adams, a preacher's wife, maybe the wife of a New York Yankee! I have surgery in the morning. Call me when you know something."

21

The next day, Cole worked in his office preparing for Sunday's sermon. His church phone rang constantly with people calling to congratulate him on his engagement. Though he did not expect to hear from New York so soon, he still flinched every time the phone rang.

Finally, at three o'clock, he gave up and went home. It was a perfect afternoon to work or run. He had just walked into his house when his phone rang. Thinking it was New York, he answered the phone. "Adams here."

After an awkward silence, a lady said, "Reverend Adams?"

Recognizing Mrs. Patterson's voice, Cole responded, "Yes, how can I help?"

"I wanted to tell you a large envelope just arrived for you."

Knowing what it was, he said, "Probably nothing, but I'll stop by in a few minutes. Just put it on my desk."

A few minutes later, he reached Tracey. "It's here. I'm home, but Mrs. Patterson at the church called to say a package from New York just arrived for me."

"Where is it now?" she asked.

"On my desk at the church."

"How long will it take you to get there?"

"I'll call you right back."

Two minutes later, Cole called back, out of breath and laughing. "You're not going to believe this. The package is from the World Council on Ministries in New York. I don't expect to hear from the Yankees until the first of next week. I'm going to get the dog and walk. See if I can forget about baseball for a while."

As he predicted, they did not hear from the Yankees on Saturday or Sunday. However, when they did not hear from the team on Monday or Tuesday, his highest expectations turned to concern.

On Tuesday morning, while shaving, Cole realized he was talking to himself.

Remember this was something we neither wanted nor went out looking for. They came after me. I'm not at all sure I would accept an offer from them. Been retired now over five years. I'm a preacher now. If they had not given me $2,500, I would have never agreed to talk to them—should not have done that.

On Wednesday morning, Josh Palmer was waiting for Cole when he reached his office.

"I should have called you. Big boss has been at an owner's meeting in Orlando over the weekend. He had to agree on the terms of this contract," Palmer said, handing Cole a package. "Look it over and let's talk. It's a one-year contract with an option for a second year. Sign the contract, and you get three million dollars; performance options are for an additional million. Pretty easy to get three quarters of the money; the rest is up to you. Questions?"

"Not sure what I expected," Cole said, opening the package. Inside were papers and a Yankees jersey. "Your offer is very generous. Thank you very much. For the moment, I have two questions: How long do I have to let you know? And what happens if I get hurt?"

"You have one week to accept or decline. Second, when you sign the contract, you get three million dollars whether you are playing or not.

My phone number is on my card, so call me when you decide what you want to do."

Just as Palmer left, Mrs. Patterson stuck her head into Cole's office. "Don't forget the building committee meeting. They're in the conference room. I fixed coffee."

Knowing he would be tied up for at least an hour, Cole left a voice mail for Tracey: "New York was here first thing. It's a good offer. I'm going to a building committee meeting now. Call back when you can."

The building committee consisted of Cole and six elders. This group also functioned as the long-range planning and budget committee. The meeting seemed to last forever. It was almost noon when the chairman summed it up: "We need to do something soon. To fix the roof is the most pressing. Though we agree the church needs an associate pastor, now is not the best time to do so. Our best course of action is to approach the bank and see if we can refinance our business loan to add in enough money to fix the roof."

***

Later, Cole had just returned from the field next to the church, where he'd been playing ball with Pete and some other kids from the youth group. He'd loaned the young pitcher his old glove. Now he returned it to its box and put the box back on the closet shelf next to his robes and the Yankees jersey that Josh Palmer had brought him. He'd spent the afternoon pondering his future—and then playing the game he loved with kids who loved it, too. *This day has put the choice ahead of me into perspective,* he thought.

Tracey had been steadily busy and finally managed to return his call from the morning.

"So sorry. It has been quite a day," she said. "Now, tell me what New York said."

"They like us," he laughed.

"How much do they like us?" Tracey asked.

"Three, four."

"What the devil does that mean? Three, four."

"I've only had a minute to study it. We can do that tonight. If I sign it—and I have a week to make up my mind—they give us a check for three million dollars.

"Over the next twelve months, we would get checks that would total an additional one million dollars. The checks would come on the first of the month. There are bonuses in addition if I do certain things like win X number of games. That's pretty much it. What do you think?"

"Think? I don't know what to think! I don't know what to say! I am simply blown away," Tracey replied. "Ten days ago, I didn't see this coming. It's a real game-changer. I'm so proud of you! I must have done a really good job when I patched up your eye. There's a lot to think about, like when are we going to get married? Let's eat in tonight, and we can talk. One last thing, there's a house on the market I would like to look at."

Cole responded, "Whoa, too much, too much. I don't think I can get my mind around matrimony, baseball, and a new house at the same time, but we'll see."

Later, after dinner, Tracey said, "Let's talk about getting married. You know married people do sleep in the same room. I expect you to snore and toss and turn, and I'm fine with that, but the dog is too much. Two of us is fine in bed but not three."

"I'm ahead of you on that one. I already bought a dog bed for him. Bit of a change, but he's getting used to it," Cole said. "Speaking of changes, this house has a lot of charm, but it's small. If I sign with the Yankees, we could easily afford a new house. What do you want me to do about the contract?"

"It certainly changes our lives for a year or perhaps two. This will give you, or us, the money to do the things we've talked about—that you've talked about—for the church. We'll be separated when the team is on the road. Both good and bad, but the good far outweighs the bad, so sign it. Do it, tonight if you can. Don't waver. Do it now," she encouraged him. "And let's get on the phone and start calling my mom and your parents and brothers and sister. See if your dad, or brothers, can come here and marry us. Let's do it quickly. The sooner, the better. Talk to Josh Palmer.

Will he keep the news of the contract signing quiet for at least a week, if possible?"

Starting the next morning, Cole's first order of business was to call Josh Palmer and become a New York Yankee. The thought of what he was about to do made him so nervous that he decided to call his father first, tell him the plan, and ask him if it was a good idea. When his mother answered, they chatted for a few minutes before his father picked up the other line.

"Rachel, don't hog the line when it's Cole," his dad chuckled.

"Hey, Dad, first item I need to talk to you about is: I need your help. When could you and Mom come to Georgia and help me get married? I'd love to have you both, plus Bill, Joseph, and Cecile. Yes. Tracey only has one sister, Sandra, who lives nearby. Like me, Sandra is a widow. Her husband, a doctor, was killed in a helicopter crash just a few months after they were married. You remember Tracey. She was the doctor who operated on my eye."

Cole's dad said, "She must be quite a girl if it takes two Presbyterian preachers to get you married."

"Not two, but three, and if I'm the one to say, 'I do,' that would be four Presbyterian preachers altogether. Hopefully, we could get married in a few weeks. If you could talk to the family for me, I have another matter to talk to you about."

Cole took a deep breath and launched into his story.

"A few days ago, a scout for the Yankees came to see me. They gave me $2,500 to let a doctor examine me and then watch me pitch. They've offered me about four million dollars to play for them one year and an option for a second year. If I sign, they give me a check for three million dollars that day."

There was a long silence.

"Dad, I know what you're thinking: I'm a preacher, not a baseball player. When I left the Cardinals after Diane died, I never expected to put on a uniform again. I didn't see this coming. Didn't want it, but this church is alive and growing. We have outgrown the sanctuary, and the roof leaks. We want to call an associate pastor, but we don't seem to have the money. We owe the bank and struggle to make the payments, and we have dreams of building an annex attached at the rear of the sanctuary that would have a gym for our young people, along with Sunday school rooms and a large kitchen," Cole said. "I can help. I know there's a reason I was sent here. If going back to baseball can make these things happen, then my number just got called. What do you think?"

"When do you have to give the Yankees an answer?" Dan asked.

"I have to let them know in six days."

"Do it. Do it today. Do it right now. I understand that you were called to minister to that church, but there are different ways to minister, and this is an opportunity you must not miss. This is something that God has given you—that strong arm of yours—and you must move ahead with this."

Cole's next call was to Luther and Pearly Mae. After a few moments of talking about the old days, he said, "Pearly, can you get Luther on the phone, and I will tell both of you a secret? If I do, will you send me a pie?"

"Well, I might if it's a good secret," she said, then yelled at her husband to pick up the other line. When Luther joined the call, Cole broke the news to both of them.

"How about this for a secret? I'm getting married."

"Oh my Lord! You don't mean it?" Pearly exclaimed, while Luther congratulated him.

"Two or three weeks, when my parents can get here. Want to know what the other secret is? You're not going to believe this, but I've agreed to return to professional baseball. I am going to sign a contract with the New York Yankees, probably tomorrow."

"Wait, wait a minute, I have a bad connection," Luther said. "You say you're getting ready to sign a contract with the New York Yankees?"

"Yes. It's a one-year contract to pitch for them, plus an option for a second year, and it's for an AWFUL lot of money."

"Mighty fine, Cole," Luther said. "Real proud of you."

"I thought you retired. You been playing somewhere?" Pearly asked.

"No, but they had me work out and put a speed gun on me and measured my fastball at 98 to 104 mph."

"Oh, my goodness! It's gonna take me a long while to digest this, but both of us are so proud of you," Pearly said. "Maybe we can get down to Georgia to see you get married."

Now Cole had one last call to make. Josh Palmer answered on the first ring. "Hey, Cole. You okay?"

"Yes, I'm fine. Talked to my family, talked to my fiancée, and prayed about your offer—bring me the papers. I'm ready to sign. Sunday, I'm going to tell the congregation."

"Well, Cole, hooray. Welcome to New York and the Yankees. You'll look great in pinstripes," Palmer said. "I only live about thirty miles from you. I can bring the papers to you this afternoon. As soon as you sign, the money will be wired to your local bank account. Does two o'clock work for you?"

With that call out of the way, Cole turned to plans for notifying the church of his decision. Josh Palmer arrived a few minutes before two, and thirty minutes later, Cole was a member of the New York Yankees baseball team. How easy it had been to sign three pages and change the direction of his life for the next nine months or so! There was an option for a second season, but only if both parties agreed to it. There would be no press release for a week to give Cole time to talk to his congregation.

Cole asked his secretary to call the six members of the church finance committee and ask them to have a cup of coffee with him in the morning. They were all in town and available. Cole wondered if they had any idea of the changes he was about to propose.

The next morning, as they were drinking coffee, Martha Franks said, “Cole, I have this feeling you’re up to something. You even have doughnuts for us this morning. You’ve never done that before. You’re not leaving us for another church, are you?”

Cole laughed and said, “Pretty good guess, Martha, but no, I love this church and all of you. What I have to tell you is entirely different. Ten days ago, a scout for the New York Yankees baseball team came here, in this office, and asked me to let a doctor examine me and then throw about twenty pitches. I refused. Three days later, he came back and offered me $2,500 to let the doctor examine me and to throw about twenty baseballs, which they would measure with a speed gun. A few days later, I was offered a contract for more money than I ever dreamed of.”

Before Cole could continue, Estelle Davis, well known for her curly wigs, interrupted him. “I knew he was leaving. I told you so. We should have increased his salary the first of the year.”

He always grinned when he saw Miss Estelle—had done that ever since Mrs. Betty Louis had reached up in church to pull a string off Miss

Estelle's neck and pulled off her wig instead. The things you see from the pulpit cannot be unseen, he thought.

"Hold on; I am not going anywhere," Cole replied. "Hear me out. What I am asking you to do is discontinue my salary on the first of the month. That will give you more than enough money to call an associate pastor, something we have wanted to do for over a year. We owe the bank, and they have a mortgage on this building. That loan will be paid off Monday morning, if you agree."

Cole held up a hand, tallying up the church's needs with his fingers.

"The roof leaks, the front of the church is deteriorating, the sanctuary is too small, and the church is growing. We need to expand the sanctuary and fix the roof. I will pay to have that done," he said. "Finally, I would hope the church would have an architect draw up plans for a new building attached to the rear of the church that would have a basketball court, at least eight Sunday school rooms along the side, and a new kitchen. Hopefully, the church can help pay for this new building; if not, I stand ready to do so. I will go to spring training in late February and will return in the early fall. This is for one year only, perhaps two. I will still be your preacher, even though I may be gone for a few months."

At first, the room was quiet; then everyone began talking at the same time.

"How did this happen?" Estelle asked.

"Is this something you've been working on?" Martha wanted to know as she laid down her pen across the church's financial statement.

"No. It just happened unexpectedly," Cole answered. "I throw baseballs every afternoon behind my house. I've done that every day since I retired from the Cardinals. It's my way of keeping fit. I even did that when I was in seminary. The only time I've actually pitched was in that game against the Baptists. That's when the Yankees' scout saw me. He was at the game because he has family here. His brother was on the Baptist team, and I struck him out. Then the scout came by church one Sunday and saw me out back showing the kids a pitch or two."

Cole took a deep breath.

"Keep this in mind. I feel like this is something God has called me to do, and I plan to do my best to do it. It does give us a wonderful opportunity to grow this church and to move ahead for decades to come."

The board members gave their blessings in support of his plan. With the meeting out of the way, Cole knew it was time to move forward. First, he headed to the bank to make sure the check from New York had arrived and was in his account. By the way the bank manager, Mark Stratton, jumped up, straightened his tie, and came to greet him, it was obvious the money had arrived. Cole couldn't remember the manager noticing him when he had come into the bank to pay the church note in the past. Now the situation had changed.

"How may I help you, Mr. Adams?" Stratton asked. "I have just heard about your return to baseball. Congratulations!"

"First, I would like for you to give me a payoff amount on the church note," Cole said. "They have been paying on it for years, long before I came here, and I assume there would be no late fees or other charges."

Stratton responded, "No, sir. No extra charges, but I ought to charge you double."

"Charge me double? Where are you coming from with that?"

"Well," Stratton laughed. "You don't recognize me with my suit on, but I was the catcher for the Baptist baseball team. We made a bet when you were at bat. I still owe your church a visit for that home run!"

"No, no. I had my mind so wrapped around these construction projects for the church, I didn't think about that. We'd be glad to see you there anytime." Cole laughed and said, "Can I still get the money?"

"Let's start over. My name is Mark Stratton, and I am honored to be your banker. You don't know this, but the whole town is proud of you. Unbelievable that someone from this town is going to play for the New York Yankees, the same team Babe Ruth and Mickey Mantle once played for. If it was up to me, we would pay you to bank with us instead of charging you. But I would like to ask you just one more question. How did you guess what sort of pitch our guy would throw when you hit the home run?"

"Well, he was pitching to a pitcher. If I had been in his place, I would have thrown a fastball, just as he did," Cole said. "Now that we're friends again, I'm going to need a construction loan secured by my money here in the bank for the church to build a new recreation area to include a dining room and several Sunday school rooms."

After finishing at the bank, Cole stopped by the real estate office next door to see if a house he had been looking at was still on the market. The agent, Harold Johnson, was a member of Cole's church and a good friend.

"No doubt, Cole," Johnson remarked, "the church parsonage is going to be a little small after you get married."

"It's already a little tight with Lucifer and me, but no way for one more person," Cole said. "When our new associate pastor comes, I need to be out of there. Are you still good to take us to look at houses this afternoon?"

"Yes, how about four o'clock? Is that a good time for you?" Johnson asked, smiling.

"Probably four thirty would be better for us."

"Good, I'll pick you up at the church. Don't bring the dog."

The house Cole had been looking at was no longer available, and by six o'clock, it was obvious there were very few suitable houses on the market. As they were heading home, the real estate agent suddenly said, "Got an idea. Would you consider a farm?"

"Not me. I'm a city girl," Tracey replied.

"And I," Cole said, "spent several hot summers in Memphis raising squash, corn, beans, and tomatoes. That was enough for me."

"I understand where you're coming from; however, it's right on the way home," Johnson said. "Won't take us a minute to look at it—less than a mile out of town." A few minutes later, they pulled up to a gravel road with a gate and a padlock.

"A good friend of mine built this place—came here with industry, got promoted, and had to move to Cincinnati—only lived here for three months after the house was completed. The house sits on roughly sixty acres of ground with a five-acre lake in front of the house."

As they pulled up to the house, two deer walked across the driveway, unconcerned with their presence. The house sat on a small ridge overlooking the lake. Fields on both sides of the road had been clipped with bales of hay stored nearby.

"Oh, my," Tracey mused. "Poor man built this place and had to leave it and move to Cincinnati. What sort of price is he asking?"

"He's dropped the price, just wants to recover his cost," Johnson replied. "Let me tell you a little about the house before we talk price.

"Walk around and look at it. The house has three bedrooms and three baths, and a large kitchen with a wood-burning fireplace that is open both to the kitchen and the living room. You'll notice the large windows, especially in the kitchen, that look out over the lake."

"You still haven't told me the price," Tracey said.

"He's willing to do it two ways, entirely your choice, sixty thousand dollars for the land, which he's willing to keep. One hundred forty-four thousand dollars for the house. Two hundred thousand if you take both."

After walking through the house, Tracey nudged Cole in the ribs and said, "Let's go into the other room and talk. Come on, Cole, you haven't said much of anything."

"This sort of caught me by surprise, but it has got our name on it."

"I'm in," she said. "I know you have the baseball money, but I've saved a ton from my practice. Tell the real estate agent we'll offer one hundred eighty thousand dollars if that includes the two deer we saw."

Two days later, their offer was accepted. The only exception was the deer, with the agent saying Tracey would have to bring that up with the deer at a later date.

Several days later, they were relaxing at the parsonage and opened a bottle of wine. "I still can't believe we found such a place," Tracey said. "We should have gone there first. I was so discouraged. No way did I expect, or hope, to find a place like that."

Cole chimed in, "Did you notice the fireplace in the kitchen? One fire will warm both the kitchen and the den, and you know how much I love an open fire. That's what sold me."

"Yes, I know," Tracey said. "I saw the twinkle in your eyes when you saw the fireplace. I was exhausted and ready to go home until I saw those two deer."

"I'm already making a list of things we need," Cole said.

"Uh oh. What sort of things?"

"Oh, you know, we'll need a tractor to keep the hay cut, a weed eater, a leaf blower, probably a riding lawn mower . . ."

"Stop. Stop. If you do all of that, we won't be able to afford the house."

"You know I'm teasing. When the grass is growing, I'll be playing baseball in New York."

"Before you start working on the yard, let's talk about the house interior. Our wedding is scheduled for less than three weeks, so we—or rather you—need to be out of the parsonage by then. That house is completely furnished. When the owner moved out, it looks like he just washed the dishes and drove away. For us to move in, he's got to move out, so to speak. Let's call the agent and see if we can help."

The real estate agent was out but called back a couple hours later. "I've been on the phone with the seller for almost an hour. Talked my ear off, but I've got an interesting proposal for you. He's been promoted and is moving to the company headquarters in Ireland. He has no use at all for the house furnishings, to include a tractor, a lawn mower, and a golf cart. What you don't want, you can throw away; however, almost everything in the house is new. He only lived there for two months or so. The price is eleven thousand five hundred dollars, which includes the toilet paper and the dishtowels. Anything you don't want, I'll help you take to Goodwill or United Way. What do you think?"

"That solves a lot of problems. Some of the china is not my first choice, but it would get us through the wedding," Cole said. "Any china and silver we don't keep could go to the church. The church has to supply everything for the new kitchen they're building, and right now they don't have anything."

Tracey added, "Some of your family or mine will probably stay here when they come for the wedding."

Cole smiled and said, "Here comes our first marital crisis, who wears the pants in the family?"

Tracey laughed, "You go play baseball, Cole. Lucifer and I say, 'Yes!'"

"Me too," Cole added. "Let's get the paperwork done."

WANDA STANFILL

A couple of weeks before the wedding, Cole was in his office looking at estimates to repair the sanctuary roof. In addition to the roof, the old heating and air conditioning system would have to be replaced. Then there was a knock at his door. Mrs. Patterson stuck her head into his office. "Cole, Reverend Bobbie Jennings is here to see you."

"Mrs. Patterson, I'm really busy trying to understand these estimates. Can you see what she wants?"

"No, Cole, I suspect you better handle this one."

Cole said, "Send her in."

He looked up at the tall redhead in the doorway. "Come in. Come in and welcome. I wasn't expecting our associate pastor for at least another month—at least, according to our hiring committee chairman."

She said, "And I'm sure I'm not what you were expecting."

Cole laughed. "Please sit down, and let's talk. First, I'm glad you're here. Welcome to the First Presbyterian Church of Denmark, Georgia. We are an active and growing church, and we are in desperate need of an associate pastor to cover for me next summer. Now tell me more about yourself. I saw the committee's report on your background, but I'd rather you fill me in."

"I am a recent graduate from seminary, Columbia, like you, and I was top ten in my class," she replied. "My friends call me Pepper because of my curly red hair. I am an Okie from Lawton, Oklahoma, where I grew up. I went to the University of Oklahoma on a fast-pitch softball scholarship. Today, I am on my way to a tournament about forty miles from here. I just wanted to meet you and see my new church. I'll be back in three weeks to start work."

Cole said, "Do you know about my plans with the Yankees?"

"Yes, that is one of the reasons I wanted to work here in Denmark," she said. "I do, however, confess to being a Boston Red Sox fan, but I'll get over that."

At that moment, there was a knock at the door, and Tracey came in. "Hey, Tracey! Good timing! This is our new associate pastor, Bobbie with an 'I-E' Jennings from Lawton, Oklahoma, and she says her friends call her Pepper because of her red hair."

Tracey said, "Pepper, or Bobbie, nice to meet you. Sure you won't be here for the wedding?"

"No, but thanks. I'm on my way to a fast-pitch softball tournament in Florida. I'll be back in three weeks. I just wanted to see my new church and my new boss."

"I hope you win," Cole said.

Later that afternoon, Tracey said, "I've never seen that many curls in a woman's hair, and bright red, too! How tall was she? About six feet?"

Cole said, "Yeah, I guess so."

"And did you see the way she handled that luggage before she left here? If I get in a fight, I want her on my side."

Their wedding day was less than two weeks away, and there remained much to be done. The ceremony, of course, would be held at the church. Roof construction would begin after the wedding, as well as the sanctuary enlargement. The reception would be at the country club. All members of the congregation were invited to both the wedding and the reception.

The next ten days flew by. Cole had one Sunday sermon, one funeral, and visitations to several elderly members of the congregation who were ill. The week before the wedding, he moved out of the little house behind the church and into the new house in the country. Tracey would move after the wedding. Plans for the new church gymnasium, Sunday school rooms, and kitchen were put on hold until after the wedding.

Two days before the ceremony, the town began to fill up with friends and family members. Tracey's mother and sister were among the first to arrive. Cole's parents, two brothers, and sister all arrived in a bunch, followed by Britches Malone, Luther and Pearly, and Mrs. Wilson and her three children. By late afternoon, they all had gathered at the new house.

Cole and Tracey were near the front door when Tracey said, "You've got a phone call. Man says it's important."

Somewhat irritated, Cole took the phone and said, "Cole Adams speaking; how may I help you?"

"Hey, Cole! Earnest Coleman here. Hope I'm not interrupting anything. I'm in charge of public relations and media events with the New York Yankees. We've been getting a lot of interest and inquiries about you and your unusual sidearm delivery. Here's the deal—we have a chance to be front-page news on a lot of New York and East Coast papers. To make the deal go down, we need you in New York by noon tomorrow. I'll have a plane at the Denmark airport by nine in the morning. Don't really think we'll need you more than a day or so. Any questions?"

"There is absolutely no way I can get to New York tomorrow."

"Cole, I don't think you understand how big this deal is."

"I really don't care. I'm sorry, but I cannot be there tomorrow."

"Cole, if you cannot do this, I'm afraid it will void your contract. We will stop payment on your check, and I only hope you haven't done anything foolish like buy a house or something."

Looking around, Cole realized that people were watching him with amused expressions. "Hey, Mr. Coleman, give me just a minute to check my schedule."

Slipping quietly to the back of the house, he found Britches Malone holding a phone with a washcloth over it to distort his voice.

"Surely, surely, I would not find my friend and best man playing such a joke on me. I should introduce you to my ferocious dog, Lucifer, or perhaps I'll just owe you one in the unlikely event you ever get married."

With much laughter and teasing, they moved to the back yard to check on the barbecue. While Cole and Tracey were outside, Nancy Wilson came looking for them with a grin on her face.

"Cole, I'm so glad you're not getting ready to get on a plane to fly to New York City."

"Yes, yes, Nancy. It was a great trick, but I'll get even with Britches for that—just give me enough time. Tracey, you will likely remember Britches and I spent several years helping Nancy raise a garden, split wood, and look after her three children, who are all grown up now."

Nancy said, "Cole and Britches saved my life for those years, Tracey. They even helped me look for buried treasure, and that is one of the reasons I wanted to be with you today. Congratulations. I wish you many years of happiness."

Handing them a box, she said, "This is something for both of you." Inside the box were two smaller boxes, one marked "Cole" and the other "Tracey."

"You go first, Tracey."

In her small box, were two small, round objects. When Tracey began rubbing them, she realized they were gold. "Oh! Oh! Cole!"

Lost in thought, Cole was looking at the gold coins in his box. "Nancy, oh, my! Is this what I think it is? Did this come from the garden? Did they come from the lost safe in the old train wreck?"

"Yes, you guessed it! We moved the garden to a different area last year. We've never planted on that side of our place. Late summer, the twins were digging sweet potatoes when these coins started turning up."

"How many of them were there?" Cole asked.

"Lots," Nancy replied. "None of these have ever been in circulation, and the mint where they were made burned down before many of them were put into circulation. They are exceedingly rare."

"Nancy, have you ever seen a price on one?" asked Britches, who just walked up.

"Coin dealers have them listed at about twenty-five thousand dollars plus per coin," Nancy said. "May the two of you have many golden years together."

"Here, here! Toast, everyone!" came the cries from people standing nearby. Everyone crowded around, wanting to see and hold the historic and valuable gold coins.

"Wait, wait, everyone! Two more things!" Nancy said. "Britches Malone was with us for those years and part of that crazy night when Cole, Britches, and I in my nightgown tackled the man looking for the coins. Britches, I know you're not getting married, but these will remind you of that night." Britches opened the package she gave him to find two gold coins for him.

"And Cole, this is for the church; may its future be as bright as these coins." Cole took the box, expecting to find two coins, but instead he found ten! With the coins was a note:

These coins were made long ago. They are a part of the past, but today they are a part of the future. Cash them in and use them to help pay for the addition to your church. For all you did for us, let us do this for you.

—Nancy Wilson and Family

Cole said, "I need to sit down for a minute. Nancy, I could never thank you enough for a gift of this size. Are you sure . . ."

Nancy laughed. "Cole, there are more coins than I could ever use. The future is more than secure for my family, but there is one last piece I haven't told you. I have been dating a man, Arthur Solomon, for the past two years. He is even wealthier than I am, but more than that, he is more than I could hope for. We plan to get married in April. Now, let's see if we can find a glass of wine."

Hours later, after almost everyone was gone, Britches and Cole, along with Tracey and her sister, Sandra, relived the evening.

"Britches, you still live in Memphis. When did you find out about the coins?"

"I've known for a while," Britches replied. "She called and said she would like to see me. I went by that afternoon, and we laughed and talked about the old days, especially about the night we caught that guy digging in the garden. Nancy said, 'Do you wonder whatever happened to all those coins?' To tell you the truth, I was so wrapped up in my baseball career, I had forgotten about the coins. Then she pulled out a shoebox full of them. When I could get my wits together, I asked her, 'Is this what I think it is?' She said, 'Not exactly.' Turns out, that was just one of the boxes. There are three more."

At first, Britches worried about her and her money.

"But she is a smart lady. The first thing she did was talk to your dad, who got her in touch with a lawyer and a bank investment officer. Her money is safe," Britches said. "Oh, she gave about the same amount to the church in Memphis. Half of it goes into building repair and construction, and the other half goes into an endowment trust fund for college scholarships. What you do with the money here is up to you."

Britches stopped and looked at his watch.

"In less than half an hour, it will be tomorrow. Let's get some rest!"

LIBERTY
1920

The next morning started well. Cole's parents had not returned to Denmark in more than twenty years. It had been his father's first church, and about twenty older neighbors and church members went to the church to have coffee with Cole's parents. An hour or so later, Nancy Wilson and her three children stopped by. The twins wanted to tell Cole how they found the coins, and Cole wanted to relive the story with them.

"Tracey wanted to be here with us this morning, but she seems to have a big afternoon planned, something about a wedding," Nancy laughed. "I bet she is at full speed by now. You're going to be busy, too, so let me emphasize to you how rare the coins are. You need to exchange them slowly—perhaps over several years. Your father's church in Memphis is doing just that and using the money for renovations, maintenance, and their endowment fund."

"Their plan to divide the money between a building fund and endowment is the plan that we will adopt, especially since we don't have an endowment fund as of yet," Cole said. "Let's walk around the building and take a look. My whole family is in the sanctuary next door, visiting with old friends, and they want to go with us."

As Cole's family and friends began to gather, it was a mixture of the past and the present. For some, it was the first time to visit the church or enter the sanctuary. For others, like Cole's parents, it was a return to the place where they were married and where Cole's father preached for the first ten years of their marriage.

When everyone gathered in the sanctuary, Cole said, "I have a surprise for you. While cleaning out some old files to make room for our associate pastor, I found an archive of old sermons preached by my father, Reverend Dan Adams. The one I am holding is the first sermon he preached here as a new minister. Dad, would you like to read it to us?"

His father laughed and said, "I expect it would be as boring now as it was more than thirty years ago. Standing here today, I well remember how frightened I was. You, Cole, have a big advantage over me in that you have that giant dog Luc to guard you and watch over you."

Hearing his name, Luc, who was sitting in his customary place by the first pew, sat up and wagged his tail happily.

Tracey joined them when the tour ended and Cole led the wedding party to the old kitchen at the rear of the church. Nancy and Pearly had conspired to cook a Memphis-style lunch there in Georgia.

After Cole blessed the food, he said, "This may be one of my last good meals."

"Get ready," Tracey replied. "It will be bread and water after tomorrow."

What a Memphis-style lunch it turned out to be! Nancy Wilson had fixed turnip greens and fried chicken, and Pearly Mae had brought hot cornbread and six strawberry and cherry pies from Memphis.

Pearly told Cole, "Don't you worry; the ice cream is on the way."

Sitting next to Cole, Luther said, "Sort of like old times, you, me, Britches, and Pearly, eating ice cream."

Dropping his voice, Luther whispered, "Look what I got Pearly." Making sure Pearly did not see what he was doing from the other side of the table, Luther pulled a box out of his coat pocket. Inside was a gold necklace, a chain with a little medallion that looked like a replica of the coins from the garden. He'd paid an artist to make the necklace, with money he'd received for one of the coins the Wilsons had given him.

"Been married over thirty years, never had money to give her something like this. Mrs. Nancy made that happen."

Tapping her glass on the table, Tracey stood up and said, "Wedding party needs to be back here in two hours. Everyone else needs to be at the country club by seven o'clock. Cole, my sister is going to stand in for me during the rehearsal—no hugs or kisses permitted."

The rehearsal went as planned. One of Cole's brothers quipped, "How could it not go well with four preachers?"

Following the rehearsal, the group gathered for dinner at the country club. After dinner, it was time for a toast. Cole started, "This is an old family toast. I only hope I can get it right:

'Here's to the one and only one
And may that one be she
And may that one have but one
And may that one be me.' "

Following a round of applause, Tracey stood up and said, "My toast is to my groom. Ten years ago, when I was a young doctor, he was my patient. After we had begun to fall in love, I said to him, 'Maybe someday.' Tomorrow is 'someday.' Here's to tomorrow. At last, it came true."

Later that evening, after the rehearsal had ended, and after many more toasts, a small group gathered at the hotel where most of the guests were staying.

"Do you ever think . . .?" Britches started.

Before he could finish, Cole interrupted. "I know what you're thinking. What if Robert Sullivan hadn't beaten me up and hurt my arm? I would never have learned to pitch left-handed."

At that point, he was interrupted by a chorus of cheers: "Toast! Toast! Here, here! Here's to Robert Sullivan!"

After several more toasts, Cole continued, "If that didn't happen, I would never have fallen under Luther's care, and how many slices of cherry and strawberry pie would Britches and I have missed? Let's have a toast to Luther and Pearly. Without them, we might be half the size we are today."

More cheers followed. Then Cole said, "Luther, there was a baseball glove I fell in love with, a red one that was all I could think about, but I couldn't afford it, and then somehow the price dropped almost in half. I still have that glove. How much did you have to give that salesman?"

"Now, Cole, it wasn't much. You don't owe me nothing, but you can give me one of your coins from the garden if you want to—that'd make us about right."

Cheers erupted. "Toast! Toast! Here's to Luther!"

"Think of all the what-ifs in our lives," Cole added. "What if I had not been hit in the eye by a baseball? I would never have met Tracey. And what if that gentleman at the restaurant hadn't thought I proposed?"

Britches added, "Here, here! A toast to that old gentleman!"

And Cole, with a sad expression, stood and said, "Here's to the headaches we're all going to have in the morning, but one last toast! It's a quarter to two in the morning. Today I am getting married, and with that, I bid you all good evening."

Shortly thereafter, it was morning. It was light outside, so it must be tomorrow, or today. This was the day Cole was getting married, and he didn't feel well. What had tasted good last night didn't taste so good this morning. *Preachers aren't supposed to have hangovers,* he thought. He didn't plan to tell anyone he felt unwell, especially on the day he was getting married.

As Cole thought about the day ahead, his thoughts drifted back to an earlier time when he and Diane had married. He was still pitching in Triple A for the Memphis Redbirds. How happy they had been! He had been called up with the Cardinals, and they were beginning to make plans to have children. Then cancer had changed their plans, and soon she was gone. How often he wondered what it would have been like if Diane hadn't gotten sick. He would have stayed with the Cardinals and not gone to seminary.

As Cole sat on the edge of the bed, he felt something pushing on his feet. Looking down, he could see that Luc was not only awake but ready for breakfast. "Okay, old friend, let's get up and get this day started. What would you like for breakfast? It's time for me to quit thinking about yesterday and get excited about today."

Reaching for the phone, he decided to check on Tracey. When she answered, Cole asked, "Hey, what are you doing today? Anything fun?"

"Cole, right now, I've got three or four patients this morning. Nothing complicated. Probably replace an eye or two, and after that I plan to get married, and after that I plan to escape and go away someplace wonderful, though I don't exactly know where."

Cole laughed. "Well, we're the second generation to get married in that old church. Let's do it right. The rehearsal went well yesterday. Luc wanted to walk down the aisle with Britches and your sister. My mother will keep an eye on him during the ceremony."

Cole was busy packing his car for a fast getaway after the wedding when Britches pulled up. After talking for a few minutes, Cole laughed and said, "You don't look so good. You look sort of green, like a frog."

"I noticed that this morning when I made the mistake of looking in the mirror. You look about the same."

As the two laughed about how they felt, Britches's phone rang. "Damn! That's the third time this morning my agent has called me. The trade deadline is today. Surely the Tigers haven't traded me. Besides, I have a no-trade clause in my contract. They can't trade me unless I agree to it."

"Call them back and get it over with so I can keep making honeymoon plans for Tracey and me to get away."

Britches disappeared into the house to call his agent. Some fifteen minutes later, he emerged with a strange look on his face. *He looks floored,* Cole thought in concern.

"Hey, Cole, I just got a pile of money. You're not going to believe this, but the Tigers just sold my contract."

"You can stop that!" Cole interrupted.

"No, I can't. I agreed to it."

"Are you telling me you are no longer a Detroit Tiger?"

"No. No, I'm not, and you can never guess who my new team is."

"It's probably the Cardinals or the Red Sox," Cole guessed.

"Wrong. Wrong. Better than that," Britches said, smiling widely and pounding a fist against his hand in an expression of excitement. "I'm going to be there with you and the New York Yankees! They will use me as a designated hitter, spare outfielder, and catcher when you pitch. I'll be your catcher! Sort of like old times!"

"Best news I could get!" Cole said, slapping his friend on the back in congratulations. "I've been nervous about going back, and that makes me feel so much better!"

"What a great day this is: signed a new contract with a team I'm excited to play for, made enough money to retire on if I wanted to, and got a date with your new sister-in-law after the wedding! And just wait till Luther hears about both of us going to be with the Yankees! Too much! Too much! Hope I can remember to make it to the church by three o'clock!"

That afternoon, the little church filled up fast. Looking at his watch, Cole realized it was nearly three thirty. He was about to be a married man once more. His heart skipped a bit with joy—and a little bit of nerves.

His father straightened Cole's tie and patted his shoulder. "It's about time to go and see your bride," he said, smiling.

The church was packed, with a number of people standing along the aisles and the rear of the old building. As the organist began playing "Trumpet Voluntary," everyone stood up, and Tracey began her walk down the aisle. Even Luc was standing and watching the aisle. After Tracey reached Cole, his father, and two brothers, the ceremony began. When the time came to exchange wedding rings, Cole slipped a ring with diamonds and sapphires onto her finger. In turn, she put a gold wedding band on Cole's finger. As the ceremony ended, Cole gently kissed his bride.

On their way to the wedding reception, Tracey whispered, "My patient, then my college sweetheart, and now my husband. 'Maybe someday' is finally today."

When they reached the country club, people who had been unable to be seated at the little church had already filled the ballroom. One of the first people Cole saw was Josh Palmer. After greeting Cole and hugging Tracey, he said, "I look forward to meeting our newest Yankee, Stevie Malone. I've heard about the joke he pulled on you."

"Give me a little while," Cole responded. "I'll get even, but for the moment, Sandra has him in a trance. Britches, come over here and meet Josh Palmer with the New York Yankees."

Cole left them talking and began shaking hands and hugging some of his close friends and congregation members while he introduced Tracey to those who hadn't met her already. When the band began to play, Cole and Tracey had the first dance while everyone watched.

Tracey whispered, "This is the wedding ring I've dreamed of. How did you know?"

"Secrets. Secrets," Cole whispered. "Maybe someday I'll tell you." As other people began to dance, Britches danced with Tracey, and Cole danced with her sister, Sandra.

"You've got Britches enthralled," Cole said.

"He's a mess," Sandra responded.

Next, Cole danced with Nancy Wilson. She glanced at Britches—who was awkwardly twirling Sandra in endless circles—and whispered, "Probably a good thing we didn't have any dance parties when you and Britches spent those summers with us."

They both chuckled at the notion of young Britches dancing. More than a little emotional, Cole replied, "I can never thank you enough for your generosity to Tracey and me, Luther and Pearly, Britches, and, most of all, to the two churches. May God bless you and your family in the years ahead."

As the song ended, Cole went to find his wife and whispered, "Let's go dance with Luther and Pearly, cut the cake, and then make our getaway."

At first, Cole could not find Pearly. The band was playing a fast number and the dance floor was full. When he found her, she and Luther were in the middle of the floor, with everyone standing and watching. Clearly, they were the best dancers there. When the song ended, Cole hugged them and said, "It's time to tell you goodbye. Don't know when I'll see you again. This summer, you be watching the Yankees on television, and you can see Britches and me in the lineup. Tell Socrates I'll be watching for him in the bigs. I'll be thinking about all of you."

At the end of the room, he found his family sitting with old friends and many new ones. Telling them goodbye, he moved toward the cake. When the band played "Take Me Out to the Ball Game," Cole and Tracey cut the cake, posed for pictures, and stepped out the door while being showered with rice and popcorn. An hour later, Cole pulled into the Bulldog Inn, where the bridal suite awaited them.

The next five days were spent in Belize in a cottage on a white-sand beach just a few yards from the ocean. One day, Cole and Tracey hired a boat and a guide and went out on the coral reefs, where they swam and snorkeled with everything from sharks to sea turtles. Though they were on the reef for hours, perhaps what they did the most was talk. They had spent years apart from each other, from that first encounter when she was a doctor and he was her patient until the day she walked into the little Presbyterian church in Denmark and Luc went to sit by her. Talking and laughing and then holding each other through periods of silence, they soon forgot about the fish swimming below.

"What if someone asked me how we met?" he said.

"Would be a little unusual for me to say I was a doctor, you were my patient, and I operated on your eye."

Then Cole said, "Who would ever believe what happened on that first date?"

"If that old man had his hearing aid in, we might not be here today. When you said, 'I propose we finish the bottle of wine,' and I accepted and he thought you proposed marriage, and then everyone started clapping and toasting us—you know what I was thinking right before that happened? It's late and I have a full load of patients tomorrow, and I really need to go home. Then you kissed me, and look what happened."

"Well, what happened? I've sort of forgotten. Let's see if we can re-create that moment." And that was the end of any talking.

After five days of paradise, with sand in their shoes and suntanned skin, they started back home. "I never thought I might say this, but I don't think I want any shrimp or crab or any other seafood for at least six months," Tracey said.

"Me too," Cole said. "I was sort of dreaming about a cheeseburger and fries myself."

Two plane trips later, plus a four-hour drive through bumper-to-bumper traffic from Atlanta to Denmark, and they were home. Sandra had stayed in Denmark to look after the house and feed Luc until they returned. As they began moving the bags into the house, Cole decided to tease Sandra. "Hey, let's get Britches to help us get all these bags back in the house."

She stopped and said, "Cole, who did you say?"

"Britches, you know Britches. He's the same one you were slow dancing with when we left for Belize."

"I know. I know who you're teasing me about. He calls me two to three times a day. Sometimes more than that. He really wants me to come to Memphis. Promised he would take me to The Peabody and Graceland. I've used up my vacation time by now. Not at all sure your wife would let me off work."

Cole laughed, "If we get to talking about Britches, it might take all day to get unpacked."

After everything was carried into the house, Tracey and her sister left to check on the new office building, which was in an old dental clinic they were rehabbing. Cole headed to town to check on the construction work at the church. To his surprise, the work had stopped.

As he looked around, Cole thought it looked like the workers had made good progress, but why did they stop? A few minutes later, the church secretary came back to his office. After a few minutes of talking about the wedding and his honeymoon, he asked, “What stopped the construction on the sanctuary?”

“They found something,” Mrs. Patterson replied.

“What do you mean, ‘they found something’? What was it?” Cole asked.

Mrs. Patterson pointed to the wall in the sanctuary. A large piece of canvas covered the wall. When Cole pulled up the canvas, he could see a yellow piece of paper taped to a small wooden box in a hole in the wall.

“Quite a way to come home from a honeymoon,” he said. “Don’t think I know what to do with this. One thing is for sure; we need to move on with the construction.”

Mrs. Patterson said, “The box will come loose if you pull on it.”

Cole tugged on the box, which slid out as if it were on rollers. “Someone went to a lot of trouble with this. Let’s see what the note says—if I can read it:

Out of the rain, out of the cold
May this box stay shut until the story is told.
Smiles and laughter, soon turned to grief
To find our pastor was naught but a thief.
With lies and deceit
His church did he cheat.
The box tells the story of a good life gone bad,
Of fighting and death and a time that was sad.

“I’m really not sure how to proceed with this,” Cole said. “Not sure if we need an archaeologist or a policeman. For starters, let’s see if we can get some members of the church finance committee to have a cup of coffee with me tomorrow, about nine o’clock. Promise them a doughnut if they come, and let’s see if Walter Thompson will join us. He knows more about our church history than any of us.”

Later that afternoon, Cole stopped by Tracey’s clinic to tell her about the box.

"I can tell you one thing," Tracey said. "I plan to be in your office at nine o'clock, so you can save a doughnut for me. No way am I going to miss this. A hundred-year-old mystery."

By nine o'clock the next morning, all six members of the church finance committee, plus Tracey, Mrs. Patterson, and Walter Thompson, the church historian, gathered in Cole's office.

Martha Franks opened the conversation. "All right, Cole, the last time you gave us doughnuts with our coffee, you told us about your contract with the Yankees. What are you up to now?"

"No, Martha. No surprise like that. Let's walk out to the front of the church and I'll show you what the problem is." When Cole lifted the cloth covering the hole and pushed out the box, he said, "Now let's take this back to my office. First, I want to read what is on the outside of the box." After reading the poem, he opened a cloth sack, and inside was a small wooden box that contained a letter, a pistol, and a knife. The date on the letter was June 30, 1864.

"Cole, I might know something about what we're going to find," Walter Thompson said. "There was a time when Union forces were here. Church records talk about a Doctor Dodson, who was a pastor. He disappeared when the Yankees moved on to Atlanta. Perhaps this box will tell us what became of him."

The letter read:

On this day, June 30, 1864, an audit of the Presbyterian Church in Denmark, Georgia, revealed a shortage of $1,760.63.

When Pastor Dodson was confronted with the shortage, he admitted to taking the money to cover gambling losses but said he had the money to repay the church. Going to his desk, he reached in a drawer and produced a small pocket revolver, with which he attempted to shoot the head of the session. Fortunately, the gun misfired, and no one was harmed. After this, he tried to escape. One of the elders, who will not be named, produced a knife, and solved the problem. A search of the pastor's desk revealed maps of Confederate positions and gun placements. Letters and documents showed that our Presbyterian preacher was not only a thief but a Union spy. Knowing the consequences if he died or disappeared, being a Union spy, the session agreed to bury him in an unmarked grave and record the incident in this manner. This document, along with the gun and knife, are to be placed in a wooden box and hidden in the church wall.

"What do we do now?" Cole asked. "We could alert the police, the state historical commission, the presbytery, or General Sherman. We can use this as part of our history. It emphasizes how long the church has been here and what a unique history this church has."

"I move to let the pastor and church historian handle the matter," Martha said.

"Somehow I felt like this would come my way, and I will handle it," Cole said.

As the group prepared to leave, Martha added, "No more surprises, Cole, my heart can't stand it."

After the group left, Cole dictated a news release to the *Denmark Dispatch*, the local newspaper:

Recent construction at the Historic Denmark Presbyterian Church has uncovered artifacts from the time when Denmark was occupied by Union soldiers as part of the Atlanta Campaign. The artifacts were found in a wooden box near the entrance of the church and were discovered by construction workers. The box included weapons and letters. The written material will be sent to the Georgia Historical Commission for study. The church, which will soon celebrate its 175th birthday, is currently enlarging its sanctuary and adding a new fellowship hall, which will include a gymnasium, dining area, and Sunday school rooms.

"I don't really want a bunch of tourists and amateur historians coming through here, especially while all this construction is going on," Cole remarked. "We will get some publicity out of this, but I want it to be the right kind. Besides, I'm not too excited about stories of a preacher getting shot or killed."

The next morning, Cole stopped by Sunshine Grocery to get a biscuit and see what the news was. One of the men seated at the so-called Liars Table called out, "Hey, Cole! Come join us and tell us about the big news at the church."

Another voice joined in. "We were going to tease you about your honeymoon, but we voted eight to nothing to wait for that. Today we want to hear about the hidden treasure found in the church."

Deciding it might be a good thing to sit down at the table before the conversation got out of hand, Cole said, "There is no treasure. Only some church documents with two related items. As you know, Denmark was occupied by Federal troops for a short time in the Atlanta Campaign. One of the Union commanders used the church as his headquarters, and these items relate to that time."

"If that's all there is to it, have you seen today's paper?"

"Don't know what's in the paper. Haven't seen one."

"Here, take a look."

Feeling a headache coming on, Cole took a newspaper and began searching for the story.

"No, no. It's on the front page, not the back."

Civil War Treasure Discovered in Denmark's Historic Presbyterian Church

Today few people are aware of Denmark's history, and yet on rare occasions, some reminder of our past is uncovered. Such was the case this past week, when construction workers uncovered a small wooden box with a letter and related artifacts that are associated with the Union occupation of Denmark in 1864. At present, state historians are studying the contents of the box. The items are expected to be on display when church renovations are complete.

"What was in the box?" one of the men said. "As usual, this article doesn't tell us anything."

"Let me explain it as best as I understand it," Cole said. "In 1864, when Denmark was occupied by Union forces, apparently the Union brought their own preacher with them. Such was the case at the Presbyterian church. Apparently, the Presbyterian preacher was a thief and a Union spy, as well as being a preacher. When a shortage of church funds was uncovered, and the preacher was confronted with it, a fight occurred and the matter was resolved."

"What happened to the preacher? Don't leave us hanging."

"When construction is completed," Cole said, "we plan to place the items on display, and you can come to your own decision. There is a lot of history in that old church. Come and visit us, and let history surround you."

With that, Cole took off before any more questions could come up.

I really don't want this to get out of hand, Cole thought. *All things considered, we are a church, not a museum. Denmark has a small museum. In a few days, when things quiet down, I will go see them. Right now, I am a few months away from spring training in Florida, and that's all I can think about.*

When Cole got home, he went to the back yard and began throwing baseballs. The Yankees had sent him a fancy new pitching target for practice. More times than not, Cole's pitches hit the target right where he wanted.

"Don't think I've lost my touch, but where I'm headed in Tampa, Florida, is another matter," he told himself.

In the weeks ahead, Cole was busier than he had expected to be. There was much to be done in the new home. Though the house was only a few months old, it had not been built to Tracey's specifications. Each day, he followed carpenters and painters around for two hours before turning to construction projects at the church.

The hole in the wall where the Civil War items had been hidden was covered up, and the sanctuary expansion would soon be finished. Plans for the new addition were complete, and bids from contractors would be finished in two weeks. The little house adjacent to the church, where Cole had lived when he came to Denmark, needed to be painted and cleaned before the new assistant pastor returned from Florida.

When all of this was done, the old dental clinic, which was Tracey's new office, needed painting and renovating. Cole was exhausted each day when he got home, but he still had enough energy for thirty minutes every other day to run a two-mile course in the fields around the house.

Some of the batters I'll be pitching to are ten years younger than I am. Don't think it'll be quite like pitching to the Baptists two months ago.

Interest in the Civil War artifacts had not diminished. One morning, Cole and Walter Thompson, the church historian, went to the library to meet with Mary O'Neal, the Denmark historical director, and Laura Hall, the museum director and Denmark librarian. After letting Mrs. Hall read the letter, Cole said, "The Union preacher was a real problem for the church. If Federal authorities knew what happened, I suspect they would have burned the church."

"Where is the body?" Mrs. Hall asked.

"Well, it would have been very convenient to simply bury him in the church cemetery," Walter Thompson replied.

At that point, an awkward silence settled. Finally, Mrs. Hall said, "What will happen to these items?"

Cole replied, "That's really why we're here today. I don't find it appropriate for the church to house them."

"Yes, I see your point, but our museum and library have very little money. It would take quite a bit, perhaps several thousand dollars, to construct an appropriate exhibit."

"Can it be done for five thousand dollars?" Cole asked.

"Yes, surely it would, but are you saying you would be willing to pay for this?" Mrs. Hall asked.

"Yes," Cole answered. "This is the best answer for the problem. Good for the church. Good for the museum. Good for Denmark."

Cole got back to the church just in time. Mrs. Patterson greeted him and said, "The new associate pastor, Bobbie Jennings, needs your help. She left her phone number. Sounds pretty important."

"Now what? Get one problem solved, and another pops up."

When Cole dialed the number, Bobbie answered on the first ring. "Cole, this is Pepper. In short, I'm in a jam. I'm about seventy miles from Denmark on the outskirts of Statesboro, and I'm broke. I had enough money to get this far, but I need help. Would it be possible for someone to pick me up? I really hated to call you, but I simply don't know what to do."

"You just stay there. I can be there in an hour. Are you at the bus station?"

"No, I couldn't buy another bus ticket so I walked to a rest stop on Interstate 16, just outside of Statesboro," Pepper replied.

"I'm heading there now."

An hour later, when Cole reached the rest stop, he saw a young woman sitting on a bag at the back of the parking lot with her head resting on a duffel bag, and she was fast asleep.

"Hate to wake you up, Pepper, but let's go home, and we might stop for lunch if you haven't eaten. When is the last time you had something to eat?"

"I'm sorry for this," she said. "I thought I had enough money, but there is something wrong with my credit card, and I haven't eaten anything since yesterday morning."

Seeing a sign that advertised the largest and best hamburger in Georgia, Cole pulled into the parking lot. Three double cheeseburgers later, Pepper fell asleep once again and did not wake up until they reached Denmark.

Relying on Mrs. Patterson to get Pepper settled, Cole turned his thoughts to church construction projects. An hour later, he was working on preliminary construction bids when his cell phone rang. Seeing it was a Memphis number, he answered, expecting to hear his mother, but instead it was Britches.

"Hey, Cole. Glad to hear you survived your honeymoon."

"Yeah, it was perfect. No telephones. No television. Just the two of us and sandy beaches and ocean. Really couldn't have been better, but now we're back to reality. Tracey is redoing the house, and I'm working on construction jobs here at the church. What are you up to?"

"Well, I've got news," Britches said. "My family here in Memphis is pretty much gone, only have a cousin or two left. Long story short, I've rented a house there in Denmark and plan to live there at least until March when we go to spring training in Tampa."

"Hey, Britches! This isn't another one of your jokes, is it? Or could it possibly have something to do with my sister-in-law?"

"I'm going to take the Fifth Amendment on that one. Just wanted to tell you to get ready. I've got my catcher's glove, and we can start working out and get ready for the Yankees."

***

Pepper quickly adjusted to being an associate pastor at the small Presbyterian church in Denmark. For the first few weeks, she followed Cole as she got used to daily routines at the church.

"Pepper, we have roughly four months to get you ready for this job before I leave for spring training," he said. "To start, on Sunday, I would like for you to take about ten minutes to tell the congregation about yourself and what led you to this church."

"That should be easy enough," she said. "How often will I preach?"

"I want you to preach and lead the worship service every fourth Sunday. You tell me when you're comfortable enough to start."

"I'm good to talk about myself Sunday morning and to be the worship leader two weeks after that," she replied.

Cole thought about how much progress had been made since he picked up Pepper in Statesboro. Four days later, he introduced her to the congregation at the regular Sunday worship service. With her robes and stole, her red hair, and standing a little over six feet tall, she was quite a striking figure.

"I am so pleased to be here and to be a part of this church," Pepper said. "Let me tell you my story. I am the only child of a single, working mother. It was tough at times. I felt like school was my best ticket out of poverty, and I made top grades in high school. Full scholarship to the University of South Carolina, top of my class there, and a full scholarship to Columbia Seminary. For the past six years, I have pitched, in my spare time, for a ladies' semipro softball team. I'll buy a steak dinner for anybody here who can hit one of my curveballs," she said, to a chorus of chuckles from the congregation.

"One of my professors took an interest in me and took me with him to church," she continued. "My Christian journey started there and ultimately leads me here today. May we walk the path of Christian love and service together in the days ahead."

***

Two weeks later, the church entered into a contract for the construction of a new family life center. Work to enlarge the sanctuary was nearly complete, and Cole had noticed several new families at the Sunday morning worship service. For the second Sunday since her arrival, Pepper led a worship service for the young people, and four new families joined the church. Life was good in Denmark.

For the first few weeks after Britches arrived, Cole did not see much of his best friend because he had signed a contract to represent a furniture company in a three-state area.

Late one afternoon, Britches appeared at the church with his catcher's mitt, saying, "Let's play ball! Pretend we're at Yankee Stadium." For the next half hour, Cole pitched, working on a curve that Britches had not seen.

"Oh! Great pitch! That ball is barely touching the bottom of the strike zone before dropping into the dirt. It would be especially tough on left-handed hitters."

"How about letting me try a couple of pitches?" came a voice from behind Cole. Looking around, he saw Pepper with a softball in her hand.

"You think you could catch a big ball like this?" she asked.

"You throw it. I can catch it," Britches responded.

With Cole watching, Pepper began throwing, easy, slow pitches at first, but then she said, "Get ready."

With that, Pepper sent off the next few pitches, and Britches responded, "Whew! I need a bigger glove for this."

"Let me show you one more before I go," Pepper said. "I call this my zero ball because nobody can hit it." The ball seemed to hang over the middle of the plate before dropping sharply to the ground.

"Whoa!" Britches said. "I can't hit that one, much less catch it. Do another one and let me watch it."

Again, the ball seemed to disappear. Cole said, "If you can do that with a softball, I should be able to do it with a baseball."

Britches laughed and said, "Maybe we should send you to pitch for the Yankees, and Cole and I will stay here and look after the church."

Cole said, "Pepper, show me how you're holding the ball. Let's see if I can do that." But the result was not the same.

"You're holding the ball tighter than I do," she said. "Loosen up a bit."

Over the next few afternoons, Cole continued to experiment with the grip, and by the end of the week, the ball began to look like the same pitch that Pepper had thrown. As Britches remarked one afternoon, "It used to be hard to hit against you. Now it's impossible."

Two weeks later, Pepper delivered the sermon during the Sunday morning worship service. Anxious at first, Cole began to realize what a natural speaker she was. When it was time for her to speak, she walked away from the lectern and down three steps to stand in front of the congregation.

With a voice that carried to the back of the sanctuary, she began, "My message this morning is 'Saying No to God.' Pastor Adams does not know this, but coming here to Denmark was not easy for me. When I finished college, I had several offers to become a part of the University of South Carolina coaching staff—offers that were very attractive, with financial security—something I had never had.

"And the prospect of seminary was unattractive, with three more years of school, learning to speak Greek, learning to speak Hebrew. I sometimes thought that just speaking good English was enough," she quipped.

"But somehow, I felt that was what I was called to do. And after graduating from seminary, still I waited and hoped God would somehow send me a message, tell me what to do. I didn't want to be like Jonah and end up in the belly of a whale, nor did I want to be like Moses and keep giving God reasons why I didn't want to follow in his footsteps. To makes ends meet and to give me time to think, I accepted an offer to pitch for a women's semipro softball team," she said. "One day, while traveling to a tournament in Atlanta, our old bus broke down here in Denmark. It's not easy to get parts for a bus that old, so we were here for many hours. Having nothing to do, I walked around town, and I was struck by the beauty of this church. With time on my hands, I came into the sanctuary and sat down. A peaceful feeling came over me for the moment or two that I was here.

"Two months later, I saw your ad in the *Presbyterian Church Leadership Connection*. If I had not experienced that quiet moment here in this sanctuary, I would not be here today. Quite simply, I felt like this is where God wanted me to be. Unlike Jonah, I did not say no. Unlike Moses, I did not think of reasons not to accept this call. What about you? What calls have you ignored or failed to hear? What do you think God is calling this church to do? Let us listen to God's call and follow the path He prepares for us."

Later, Tracey said, "What did you think of Pepper's first sermon?"

"One thing is for sure; nobody slept through it. I talked to several people who liked the message. For the first time, I'm beginning to feel comfortable about being away for six or seven months."

***

As soon as Thanksgiving was over, Tracey and Cole packed their bags and left Denmark to go Christmas shopping in Atlanta and visit family and friends in Memphis.

Britches volunteered to keep Luc for a week. Pepper said she could handle things at the church, and they were free to go. Atlanta was ablaze with brightly lit Christmas displays. Tracey was an experienced shopper, and by the end of the second day, much of their shopping was done. Early on the third day, they headed for Memphis, her first visit there.

"Tell me what you think Memphis will be like," Cole said.

"I expect to see the Mississippi River, cotton fields, The Pyramid, and lots of people going around dressed like Elvis."

"Pretty good," Cole laughed. "I'm not sure about Elvis. Sort of think he has 'left the building.' But there are other things there. I would like to show you where I pitched for the Redbirds, and then we could walk across the street and have lunch at The Peabody Hotel."

"Sounds great to me. You'll make a wonderful tour guide."

When they reached Cole's parents' home, his mother was waiting for them with a home-cooked meal. A few minutes later, his father and Cecile arrived, saying, "What's for lunch?"

Later, when they took their luggage upstairs to Cole's old room, he said, "Wow. Pretty exciting. I've never had a girl in this room before. Let's go see Nancy Wilson first, and we can look in the garden and see if she missed any coins. After that, I hear Luther wants to talk with me before I start training. Maybe Pearly will have a pie for us."

When they reached the Wilsons' house, she was waiting for them with all three of her children—James, Sarah, and Chrissy. They wanted to take Cole and Tracey out to the garden to show where the coins had been found.

"It's a wonder that the coins weren't damaged by the fire," Nancy said. "We may not understand why, but I do believe that we were meant to find them. Think of the good they are doing in both your church and your dad's."

With a bit of nostalgia in her voice, Nancy added, "You know, Cole, I am going to miss this little house. When I get married in April, I am moving. James has his own place now. Sarah and Chrissy will be staying here, but they don't have the time for a garden these days. I wish you could be here for my wedding, but I know you will be playing baseball by then."

Tracey and Cole's next stop was to visit with Luther and Pearly. When they knocked on the door, a loud voice responded, "Who is it? Don't nobody live here. Go away!"

Laughing, Cole said, "That's okay, Socrates. I had a nice present for you, but I'll just keep it."

The door opened. All smiles, Socrates ushered them inside. "You know I was just foolin' with you. Where is it?"

From his coat pocket, Cole produced a baseball, on which was written, *For my friend, Socrates. Cole Adams—NY Yankees.* Socrates, who at twenty-six was now as tall and broad as Cole, led the way toward the kitchen. Cole could smell something wonderful. After hugs and laughter, Tracey and Pearly stayed in the kitchen, while Luther, Socrates, and Cole got comfortable in the front room and talked about baseball. Socrates had been in the minors for a while, and was thinking it was time to move on. He had a degree in education and was thinking of teaching.

Socrates and Luther had been talking about Cole, Luther told him.

"I used to be a Braves fan. Then, when you pitched for the Cardinals, I switched to them and stayed for Socrates. Now I guess I'm gonna be a Yankees fan. Been studying their roster. For a team that is picked to win the pennant, their pitching is mighty thin. Do you know why they went after you? If one or two of their pitchers comes up with a sore elbow, they're in mighty deep water. They have to have you. You might be their best hope.

"Here's where I'm going with this; you're not as young as you once was. Please, pace yourself. Six months and 150 games is a lot. Your arm needs to be as strong in September as it is in April. Pearly and I are comin' to New York in August to see you play. Already have box seats behind the Yankees' dugout. Britches will take care of you, but you take care of yourself. Now, let's go eat some pie."

Cole left Tracey at home and made one more visit to the Big Boys Boxing and Self-Defense Club. Freddy, older and grayer but still as fit as ever, was sitting in the same place he had been when Cole met him nearly twenty years ago.

"Well, looky here," Freddy said. "I knew we should have kept the door locked."

Three other men were sitting around, talking and laughing. Cole felt they might be the same ones he remembered.

"How's Luther? Is he still above ground?"

Laughing, Cole said, "Well, he seemed fine when I last saw him about an hour ago. What do you know about Robert Sullivan? Last I heard he was about to have a big title fight in Berlin."

Seeing an unusual look on Freddy's face, Cole started to turn when two muscled arms wrapped him in a bear hug. Trying to turn around, he could not move. "Could that be you, Wormy? Surely not. This will be my best chance ever to put a whooping on a preacher."

"Oh, me. I should've known better than to come here. Apparently the prodigal has returned."

Laughing as he released Cole, Robert said, "Did you come here to sign up for lessons?"

"No, I came here to see Freddy and ask him about you. How are you? What are you doing here in Memphis?"

"Look around you. See any difference?"

Glancing around the building, Cole realized nothing was the same except the chair on which Freddy was sitting. Scattered throughout the club were more than two dozen young men and several young women punching bags, skipping rope, and boxing. "What a change! Tell me what is happening here. The only familiar thing I recognize is Freddy."

"I won my big fight in Berlin," Robert said. "I took my prize money, came home, and retired. The next thing, I came here and bought this old club and turned it into a place where young people learn how to take care of themselves, not only with fighting, but also with exercise and nutrition. Right now, I have almost a hundred people using the club. Now, tell me about yourself. Heard you were going back, putting on the uniform again, and is that a gold ring I see on your finger? And tell me about Britches. Come sit down."

"I came here to see about you," Cole replied, as they pulled a couple of chairs closer to Freddy. "You know I made it to the big leagues and pitched for the Cardinals for a couple years. I married a Memphis girl who was a nurse at St. Jude. Lost her to cancer after two years. After that, I sort of lost interest in baseball and quit. Came back here and got into seminary—sort of a family thing. To be honest, I did that because I didn't know what else to do."

Cole leaned forward on his chair.

"Somewhere between my second and third year of seminary, I really began to feel God's presence in my life—turned me around, so to speak, and put me on track to minister a church in Denmark, Georgia."

Cole filled them in on Tracey, about catching up with her years after she'd fixed his eye and about their recent wedding.

"I still work out a lot, and one day a scout for the New York Yankees offered me a good bit of money to pitch for one year," Cole continued. "A lot of what they pay me will go into fixing up the church. Very strange. Never thought I would go back to baseball. Seems like that is the path God wants me to take, but enough of that. What about you?"

"You would never have known this, but when we were kids, I was a bully to you because you had something I did not have—a family," Robert said. "Brothers and sisters. A mother and father. I was raised by an uncle who really didn't want me.

"After our second fight and you told me about this place, it turned me around. Freddy took an interest in me and taught me how to fight. Treated me more like I was part of his family and continued to coach me through eleven pro fights. I retired undefeated. It's sort of funny, Cole. You're the only person who ever beat me. When I retired, I had enough money to come here and buy this boxing club. Now Freddy can train all these kids you see," Robert said, clearly proud of the legacy he and Freddy had built.

"For all of this, I owe you. If you hadn't sent me here, I don't know where I might be today. But maybe you owe me, too. What if I hadn't knocked you down and hurt your arm? Turned you around and made you left-handed? I guess we owe each other."

"Sort of a funny way to look at it," Cole concluded. "But think how often bad things turn into blessings."

As Cole turned to leave, Robert put his arm around him and said, "Take care of yourself, old friend. I'll be watching for you on television."

Later at dinner that night, Tracey laughed and said, "Are you ready?"

Caught by surprise, Cole said, "Ready for what?"

"We've done what we came here for, visited family and friends, and I sense you're ready to go home."

"To be honest, I was thinking about Denmark and all of the construction projects we have."

Tracey smiled. "I want to go home and see about our home and the work on my new clinic. Let's go home in the morning."

When they got to Denmark, Tracey said, "Oh! What was I thinking? The holidays are almost here, and we've got painters and carpenters everywhere." But despite her apprehension, the work on her office was soon finished, and the painters promised to be through with their house by the week before Christmas.

At the church, work on enlarging the sanctuary and putting on a new roof was almost complete. In many ways, the old church was the same, but in some ways, it was different. When Cole first began preaching in Denmark, there were no children's sermons, and there were very few young people in the congregation. Now when Pepper or Cole did a children's sermon, it looked like a thundering herd with all the children coming up front.

A couple of weeks before Christmas, the church served a meal to about thirty homeless people. Tracey and her sister, Sandra, along with Britches and Cole, helped serve.

As they served, one of the men said, "Nice to see you again, Cole. Doubt if you remember me."

Cole smiled and asked, "Where did I know you? You look very familiar."

"I'm not sure when. Played ball with you a little while. Came up to St. Louis the same time you did. You made it. I didn't. Hurt my hand after that and been bumming around the country ever since."

Cole said, "You played second base. Was your name Bob White, like a quail?"

"You got it. Didn't think you would remember."

"How did you hurt your hand?"

"I put my fingers around a whiskey bottle and could not let go."

"Never heard it expressed quite like that before. Are you sober now?"

"Yes. Haven't had a drink since Thanksgiving two years ago."

"Well, congratulations," Cole said. "Is there any way I can help you?"

"I have money and a roof over my head. I'm looking for work, not much out there."

"I might be able to help. Come by my office in a couple of days and we will see what we can do."

"Who was that?" Tracey asked.

"A fellow I used to know in the past when I played for St. Louis. Needs a job. He may show up again. We'll see."

Two days later, Bob White stopped by Cole's office. Luc was sitting under Cole's desk. When Bob came in, the dog began growling. Surprised at Luc's reaction, Cole offered Bob a seat. The dog continued to growl until Cole said, "If you have a resume or a list of past employers, I'll see what I can do."

"I'll bring it by in a day or two."

After he left, Mrs. Patterson, the church secretary, stuck her head in his office, "That man had such an odor of whiskey, it almost made *me* drunk."

"Well, Luc didn't like him," Cole said, thoughtfully. "Why don't we check with Mike Shirley at the police department?"

A few minutes later, Chief Shirley was on the phone. "Don't be scolding me, Cole. I haven't missed church since September."

"You have been above reproach. But right now, I need your help. Are you familiar with a man named Bob White?"

After a pause, the chief said, "Where are you?"

"I'm in my office here at the church. Why?"

"Lock the doors and don't let anyone in until I get there. Call Tracey and tell her the same story. Do it right now. I'm on my way."

A few minutes later, Chief Shirley was in Cole's office. Wasting no time, he began, "Bob White is trouble, Cole. He's been in prison twice in Atlanta for felony assault. Last night there was a robbery and assault at Pops's Liquor Castle. Got whiskey and money. Pops tried to stop him, and that's when someone hit him in the head with a hammer. He described the robber. The store has a good camera. Took his picture. Do you recognize anyone?"

He showed Cole some printouts with a clear image of the suspect.

"No doubt," Cole said. "That is him. He was here in my office thirty minutes ago. Mrs. Patterson told me he smelled like whiskey when he was in her office. He is supposed to come back with a resume. What should we do?"

Before Chief Shirley could answer, Mrs. Patterson stepped into Cole's office. "He's still here! I just saw him out back!"

As they ran toward the back of the church, they could hear Luc barking and a woman yelling. When they reached the construction area behind the church, they found Pepper and Luc well in control of Bob White, who was lying on the ground, trying to surrender. She'd seen him sneaking out of the sanctuary with his arms loaded with their collection plates and a donation box they kept in the entryway.

"I yelled for him to stop, he yelled something not worth repeating, and I tackled him," she said. "And then Luc came to the rescue. Who is this guy?"

Chief Shirley handcuffed Bob White, and within minutes, another police car had arrived to take him away. The chief stayed behind to take statements.

"I expect he will be in jail for the rest of his life if he is convicted for the robbery and assault on Pops," Chief Shirley said. "We ought to deputize Luc and Pepper."

"I may deputize them to work on people who nap in church," Cole responded.

As life returned to normal, the rush to finish Christmas shopping returned. To Cole, it seemed as if Christmas came the week after Thanksgiving. The church was covered with pine branches, garlands of holly, and clusters of magnolias. A nativity scene and a large Christmas tree were at the front of the church.

Tracey and Cole agreed they would limit their presents to each other to one small gift, and then Tracey laughed, "Well, maybe we should figure on one or two more!"

Cole laughed, too, content knowing that he already had bought and wrapped six presents for her.

The sanctuary was full for the five o'clock Christmas Eve service.

Much of the church was filled with children eagerly anticipating what presents would be under the Christmas tree in the morning. Again at eleven in the evening, the church was full, this time with adults.

Christmas Day dawned cold and clear with the temperature hovering around the freezing mark. Christmas dinner would be served at Tracey and Cole's home at two o'clock. Sandra and Britches arrived at noon, followed by Pepper. Cole had a new model softball glove for Pepper, and she surprised them with a painting she had done of the church.

There was much anticipation about what Britches had for Sandra. For weeks, Tracey had been guessing Sandra might get a ring for Christmas. When she opened the package, Britches was already on one knee ready to propose. As Tracey had guessed, it was a beautiful engagement ring. To no one's surprise, Sandra cried and said, "Yes!"

Cole produced a punchbowl filled with eggnog, and toast after toast followed. A few minutes later, Tracey said, "Cole, I do have one more present for you."

The gift was small with a silver ribbon.

"We're not getting engaged again, are we?" Cole laughed.

"You have no idea what I'm giving you, do you?"

"No, I have no idea," Cole said. When at last he opened the package, there was a small silver baby rattle inside with the letter *A* engraved on it. Caught by surprise, Cole could say nothing. Finally, with one arm around Tracey, he managed to say, "Most wonderful Christmas present I ever received."

Congratulations followed along with more eggnog. A few minutes later, there was a knock on the door. As Tracey opened the door, they could hear, "God rest ye merry gentlemen, let nothing you dismay . . ." coming from the front yard. It was the church choral group, who came in for a cup of eggnog after singing a couple of hymns.

Finally, Christmas dinner was served with turkey, ham, and shrimp from the Gulf Coast. Plum pudding for dessert with bowls of fresh fruit followed. It had been quite a day. Sandra and Britches were still holding hands, and Pepper was trying to stay awake but losing the battle.

Tracey, who had skipped the eggnog, whispered, "After we get the

Christmas decorations down, we need to start getting ready. Remember, we've only got about six weeks to finish the baby's room before you leave for spring training."

Tracey was correct. Time flew by, and yet much of the work on the baby's room was finished by the first of February. Of course, the final painting could not be done until they found out whether the baby was a boy or a girl.

The week before he and Cole left for Florida, Britches said, "This is the first time I've ever gone to spring training when I'm not so excited about it."

"It does seem odd," Cole admitted. "I remember how excited I was my first time, even though I knew I would probably end up pitching for Memphis rather than St. Louis."

The Yankees were expecting pitchers and catchers to report a week before the rest of the players, so Cole and Britches prepared to depart for Tampa on the twentieth of February. The night before they left, Tracey and Sandra fixed a farewell dinner of lobster and soft-shell crab.

Britches and Cole had arranged to meet at the church at nine before heading to Tampa the next morning. When Cole pulled up to the church, he was in for a surprise. The entire front of the church was covered with ribbons, balloons, and signs that proclaimed, "World Champion New York Yankees." It seemed like the entire town had turned out for the sendoff. Along with coffee and water, the ladies of the church had baked cupcakes that looked like baseballs.

Pepper was on the front steps with a sign that said:

Denmark Presbyterian Church
Home of Cole Adams: The Pitching Preacher.

Finally, just before ten o'clock, Cole and Britches pulled out and headed for Florida. By late afternoon, they were in Tampa, where signs proclaimed, "George M. Steinbrenner Field: Winter Home of the New York Yankees." Near the front of the stadium was a sign that said, "Welcome, Players! Report Here." A young woman welcomed them and gave them a choice of available housing. Both players selected suites with waterfront views. The next morning, they were at the stadium by nine, and they found lockers with their names on them and uniforms inside.

Spring training with the Yankees was similar to spring training with the Cardinals. Everything was fresh and new, with all the hopes for a new season and none of the disappointments. Cole settled quickly into a routine of running and exercise drills before pitching with coaches watching him. Cole soon discovered he was somewhat of a curiosity. The players had heard about him, but none had seen him pitch.

It was not until the second week that he pitched against a team of rookies and minor-league players. In three innings, he only allowed one hit. The pitching coach laughed and said, "Pretty good. Pretty damn good. These poor rookies are trying to make the team, and you're pretty rough on them." At the end of the second week, Tracey came to join him for ten days. When he wasn't pitching, they would walk on the beach and talk about the baby.

Cole's first real test came near the end of the third week when the Atlanta Braves came to Tampa for an exhibition game. Britches, who would be catching, said, "Better be sharp. These are their regular players—no rookies."

The pitching coach said, "Give me five innings if you have it in you."

Cole's response was simple and direct. "Give me the ball, and let's see what happens."

Perhaps it was the time of year, early in the season when the pitchers are ahead of the hitters. For whatever reason, Cole got the best of the Atlanta hitters. At the end of five innings, the Braves did not have a single hit.

The pitching coach said, "I'm not sure what to do with you. You're as sharp as you'll ever be, and the start of the season is still three weeks away. Rest your arm, and I don't expect you to pitch again for at least four or five days." When Cole came back into the locker room, there was a sign on Cole's locker that said, "Cole Adams: The Pitching Preacher."

When the team went north to begin the season, Cole had a chance to return to Denmark for three days to be with Tracey and check on her health. He hoped to listen to the baby's heartbeat and maybe feel a little kick. After he assured himself that Tracey and the baby were fine, then he would see how construction on the church family life center was coming.

On the second morning that Cole was home, his phone rang. A cheerful voice said, "Didn't wake you up, did I?"

Laughing, Cole said, "No, Luther. How are you and Pearly doing?"

After talking about the baby for a few minutes, Luther said, "What about the Yankees' pitching staff?"

"Like most teams at the beginning of the season, we have a full staff, but it's a long season. We're okay as long as we all stay healthy. Today, we're good enough to win. If we start losing pitchers, I don't know how we'll do."

"Do what I told you—take care of your arm, and remember, Pearly and I are looking forward to seeing you later in the season."

Two days later, Cole caught a plane to New York, and soon it was opening day of the regular season. When Cole entered the locker room, he could feel the presence of the Yankees players who had come before him. Names like Babe Ruth, Lou Gehrig, Joe DiMaggio, and Mickey Mantle were the first he thought of, along with dozens of others who had worn the Yankees' uniform.

Excited fans occupied every seat, filling every inch of the stadium, and some were even in standing room only in the bleachers. After the players were introduced, the mayor of New York sang the national anthem. Cole and the other pitchers retired to the bullpen.

It was not until late in the third game of the season that Cole got the order to warm up. However, the next batter hit into a double play, and the game ended before he was needed, and so it went for the first months of the season.

The Yankees had a strong group of pitchers, especially the starters. In mid-July, Scott Brown, the number two starting pitcher, went down with a sore elbow and was lost for the season. Another pitcher came down with a bad shoulder two weeks later. It wasn't only the pitchers. The Yankees were getting hammered with injuries, which showed in their game—exactly the situation Luther had predicted.

Several players were called up from the triple-A affiliate in Norfolk, but they were of no help. On the first day of August, Cole was sitting in front of his locker reading a letter from Tracey, when one of the players said, "Skipper wants to see you in his office."

When Cole walked in, manager Thompson and the pitching coach were talking.

"You need me, Skip?"

"Yes, you've been a great help to us, Cole. For now, far more than I expected. Now we've got about five weeks left and then the playoffs, and, if we make it, the World Series. When is your baby due?"

"Three weeks from now. The twentieth of August is the due date."

"I can't let you go. Absolutely depend on you. However, we leave for the West Coast on the fifteenth. When we leave for the coast, two weeks from now, I suggest you head for Georgia. When we get back on the twenty-fifth, I need you back here, in uniform, and ready to pitch. Is that agreeable to you?"

"Yes, sir. I'll be ready when you get back." Feeling relieved, Cole walked out on the field, where he ran into Britches and told him about his plans to return to Georgia.

"Wish I could go with you. Seems like forever since I've seen Sandra,"

Britches said. Just then, several fans right behind the dugout began yelling at them.

"Oh, wow! We've got trouble now. Look who is here."

There in the front row behind the dugout were Luther, Pearly, and Socrates. After hugs and laughter, they got one of the players to take pictures of the five of them together.

"How is your bride? Are you a papa yet?" Pearly asked.

"No, not yet," Cole said. "I'm going back to Georgia on the fifteenth to be with them."

"How is your arm?" Luther asked.

"Good. Just like you predicted, we are razor thin right now. We'll be lucky to get past the Angels today. If I find y'all a uniform, can you help?"

"Put me in, Coach," Socrates joked, even though he wasn't a pitcher.

"Not me," Luther laughed. "About thirty years too late for that."

When the game started, Cole sat down in the bullpen and prepared to relax. He had pitched three innings yesterday and did not expect to be called on today. Things fell apart quickly, and it looked like the Yankees pitchers were throwing batting practice. Midway through the fourth inning, the Angels led 2–0 and threatened to score more with the bases loaded.

Almost asleep in the warm sunshine and thinking about Tracey and the baby, Cole heard his name called. The bullpen catcher said, "Get ready quick! If we lose this game, they'll be tied with us for first place."

With almost no warm-up, Cole jumped up and walked out on the field to the pitching mound.

"Sorry, Cole, but right now you're about all I got. Do your best." And with that, the manager handed Cole the ball.

Even above the rest of the crowd, Cole could hear Luther and Socrates screaming, "Strike him out!" That is exactly what he did, and then the next batter flied out and the inning was over.

When Cole walked into the dugout, the manager said, "See if you can last a couple of innings."

It didn't work out that way. Cole pitched the rest of the game, allowing only two hits. The Yankees rallied and won the game, 8–2, and Cole gave the game ball to Socrates. After staying a few days to sightsee and visit with Cole, Luther, Pearly Mae, and Socrates headed to Memphis.

A couple of weeks later, Cole caught a plane to Atlanta, where the Yankees had arranged for a car to pick him up and drive him to Denmark. It was the same driver who had picked him up months ago, when he had his initial tryout with Josh Palmer. Cole got home just before midnight.

Two days later, as they were preparing dinner, Tracey said, "The keys are by the back door. I have my bag, and we need to go to the hospital—right now!"

Fifteen minutes later, Tracey was admitted to the hospital, and Sandra arrived to help a few minutes afterward. Six hours after that, just after midnight, with Cole and Sandra watching, a red-faced, eight-pound little boy joined the party. When Cole held the baby, he let out a scream.

"He wants to go back where he came from," Sandra laughed. The little boy was perfect. "The only problem is, he looks too much like his papa."

"Maybe he'll grow out of it," Tracey teased.

Long before the baby was born, Tracey and Cole had settled on names. If the baby was a girl, she would be named for Tracey with a middle name of Bond, which was a family name. If the baby was a boy, he would be named Luther Cole Adams. On the third day, they brought the baby home, and Cole had a few more days to hold him before returning to the Yankees.

When Cole called Luther to tell him about the baby, Pearly said, "What is the child's name?"

"Well," Cole laughed, "we've put a real burden on him. His name is Luther Cole Adams. We plan to call him Luke."

A long pause followed, and finally Luther said, "My Lord. Have you named that baby for you and me? With a name like that, you reckon we can teach him how to throw a baseball?"

There was silence for a moment, and then Pearly came on the line.

"Is he okay?" Cole asked.

"Yes, something wonderful. Luther don't want you to know it, but he's crying like a baby. Send pictures as soon as you can."

Being home for a few days gave Cole time to see how the church building projects were progressing and how Pepper was doing as the senior staff member in his absence. One day, Josh Palmer came to see him. After talking about little Luke Adams for a few minutes, the two men turned their conversation to baseball.

"Let me make a prediction," Palmer said. "We have all the talent to pull off a title, but the team has been up and down this year. The Red Sox are defending their World Series title from last year, but they're not the same team as last year. The Rays are the team to beat in the American League. The World Series will be different. The Phillies are the best team in the National League. They will be tough. They aren't like the team you pitched against back in April. I expect they will be the favorite to take it all. What about you? How is your arm? Are you ready to go?"

"Yes. I am rested and ready. I can't vouch for the rest of the team, however. The injuries this season . . . our guys have spent more time battered than batting."

"That's not what I was hoping to hear. Now let me mention one more thing. You know the Yankees will want you to play for them again next year. You've been much better than they expected. Not looking for an answer now. Wrong time for that. One thing to consider, though, if you come back, the money should be twice as much as what you got this year," Palmer said. "I got to run. I'll see you next week in New York."

Cole's first thought was not to mention any of this to Tracey.

Wrong time. No need to worry her, and besides, I'm certainly not ready to commit to another year in baseball, no matter how much money they offer.

Feeling a headache coming on, Cole decided to go home and check on Tracey and the baby.

Two days before he departed for New York, his secretary stuck her head in Cole's office and said, "There's two men and a lady who would like to have a word with you."

When the trio entered Cole's office, he remembered seeing them in church the previous Sunday.

After they introduced themselves as John Talbot, Jerry Raines, and Elizabeth White, the woman said, "Cole, we are part of a search committee from the Orlando Presbyterian Church. Our ministry is carried on beyond the church wall and throughout much of Florida by radio, television, and social media. "We know you will soon leave for New York but wanted to give you some material before you go. In short, we want you to consider coming to Orlando."

Before Cole could reply, Jerry Raines handed Cole a large envelope and shook his hand as they stood to leave. "We believe the information on our church speaks for itself. Hope you'll consider us!"

While Cole struggled to get his thoughts on baseball, and off of Orlando, the phone rang. It was Britches. "Hey, buddy, when are you coming?"

"Two more days, and I'll be putting on a uniform," Cole said.

"Well, hurry up—we really need you. The Rays are coming on the first. See you soon."

Two days later, the same driver picked Cole up at nine in the morning to take him to Atlanta, where he caught a plane back to New York. Cole found it difficult to leave Tracey and little Luke, although he knew he would be back in a couple months. He also found it hard to leave Denmark. In the time Cole had lived there, he had come to love the town. With this in mind, Cole found the idea of moving to Orlando was like moving to a foreign country, and he decided to turn down the offer from the Florida church. He'd just left Denmark and was already looking forward to coming home.

***

The regular season was winding down, and the Yankees were playing better than they had all year. Cole was glad to see it, but he suspected it was too little too late. He was less and less sure that New York would even land a playoff berth—let alone a title.

On September 21, the Yankees played and won their final game at Yankee Stadium against the Orioles. It would be the last game played at the storied venue. Next year, the team would be moving on to its newly built home. After the game, with the song "New York, New York" setting the tone, the team circled the field and saluted the fans as they said goodbye to the old ballpark.

Two days later, the Yankees' World Series dreams were crushed.

They had just beaten the Blue Jays, had played well, when they got the news. The Red Sox had beaten the Indians, clinching their own playoff spot and knocking the Yankees out of contention. It was the first time since 1993 that the Yankees had missed the postseason. Cole, Britches, and their teammates were devastated. Leaving the ballpark after the Blue Jays game, Britches eyed the players walking ahead of them and said to Cole, "Unbelievable that a team with this much talent is going home so soon."

"Injuries got us all season," Cole said. "But other teams had injuries, too. We should've overcome all that. We've got a deep bench—that's why I'm here, really. Can't begrudge the Red Sox. Guess they just worked harder than we did."

Frustratingly, they couldn't go home just yet. Even with no hope of making it to the playoffs, they had more games to finish. They wrapped up the Blue Jays series and headed for Boston to play a three-game series against the Red Sox, whose run at the title had ended their own.

The Yankees took the field with something to prove.

They took the lead early and never looked back. The Yankees had the game well in hand when Cole came in to relieve a starter with a sore shoulder.

The next batter for the Red Sox was a big first baseman, Tony Clarkson, who was known not only for hitting home runs but also for starting fights. Cole's first pitch was a sharp curveball that caught the edge of the strike zone as Clarkson jumped away from the plate. The next pitch did the same thing, and Clarkson yelled angrily at Cole. The last pitch was a fastball on the outside of the plate for strike three. Clarkson acted as if he were about to charge the mound, then stopped and yelled, "Next time, Adams!"

The Yankees delivered a 19–8 knockout win over the Red Sox, but it wasn't much comfort to the team still stinging from their postseason elimination.

Sports pages the next day declared in large headlines: YANKEES DON'T GO DOWN WITHOUT A FIGHT.

The next day's game was rained out, and a day-night doubleheader was planned for the following day. Cole was told to be rested and ready.

The afternoon game was less of a rout.

Once again, Cole faced off with an angry Clarkson. Two strikes in, Clarkson spit on the ground and muttered something Cole's way. Cole didn't hear and didn't care. *I'll shut him up with another strike,* Cole thought, and then he did just that. Clarkson stomped away in a fury.

The Yankees won, 6–2, and headed for the clubhouse to get ready for the second game of the doubleheader that evening.

Between games, Cole found a moment to call Tracey. It seemed like half of Denmark had gathered at their home to watch the game on TV, Tracey told him. His mother and sister were still there. They had driven over from Memphis to help Tracey with the baby after Cole left in August. Denmark's mayor, police chief, church friends, and even some members of the Liars' Table came. Sandra was there cheering for Britches. Tracey texted him a blurry photo of Pepper holding a sign. He couldn't make out what the sign said on his cell phone, and Tracey told him it read:

Cole Adams
Our Pitching Preacher

The last game did not go the Yankees' way.

Cole was tired but ready to pitch if needed. He had barely gotten settled in the bullpen when things took a bad turn. The Yankees' starting pitcher hit the first Red Sox player and walked the next.

"Oh, no," Cole muttered.

The next pitch was inside and high, catching the batter on the left shoulder, sending him to first base, and loading the bases. The Yankees called a timeout to give another pitcher time to warm up. When play resumed, the Red Sox left fielder hit a line drive just inside the left-field foul pole for a home run.

Again calling timeout, the Yankees manager changed pitchers. "Just hold them, Cole; give us time to catch up."

Cole struck out the first two batters he faced, and the third batter grounded out. The inning was over, but the damage had been done. Twice, New York loaded the bases but failed to score. The Yankees managed to get runners on base in later innings but could not advance them.

The Red Sox had won, 4–3.

The Yankees were done for the season.

Later, as Britches and Cole walked toward the team bus, something walloped Cole in the back and nearly knocked him down. He stumbled into the team bus and turned around. Clarkson, the first baseman for the Red Sox, had rammed into Cole from behind.

"That game teach you a lesson, Preacher?" he snarled. "I'll send you an autographed picture when we win the World Series again."

Britches and some of their teammates gathered around.

"C'mon, man, that's enough," someone said to Clarkson.

Cole didn't say anything. Clarkson charged toward him again, aggressively, and Cole wasn't sure whether Clarkson meant to shove him or punch him. Either way, he didn't get the chance. Cole faked a right and hit Clarkson with a left, breaking his nose.

It was a fight like one that took place years ago.

At Yankee Stadium the next day, Cole was gathering his things and reflecting on the season. He had done all that he could for the team, more than what was expected.

Cole wanted to be part of a World Series team as much as anyone on the field. Still, the season's early end meant he was that much closer to getting home.

But what now, what next? If New York had won, he could have gone home, resumed his life in Denmark, and told baseball goodbye. Now, he wasn't sure what the future had in store for him.

As Cole finished dressing, one of the coaches said, "The manager wants to talk to you before you go."

When Cole stepped into the office, he found the Yankees manager relaxing behind a desk and smoking a cigar. "Come in, Cole, pardon the smoke. Win or lose, I smoke one cigar a year when the season is over. Thank you for being a part of this team. I wish we could have won—

perhaps next year. But the reason we got this far is because of you. I know that, and the team does, too. Thank you for wearing the Yankees' uniform.

"The Yankees will add some pitching depth to the roster. If you choose to come back, I can promise one thing for sure. We're going all the way next year. Now go catch the bus to the airport."

Coming home was wonderful. No more airplanes, no more hotels. And best of all, his family was waiting for him. Cole knew that if New York had won the World Series, there would have been a large celebration when they got home. For Cole and Britches, life soon returned to normal.

Tracey's eye clinic was growing faster than expected and would soon need more space. The baby was growing quickly and would soon crawl.

Britches and Sandra set a wedding date of November 1. Many of the people who had come to Denmark for Cole's wedding would return for Britches's ceremony.

Cole quickly slipped back into his old routines at the church. Pepper seemed especially glad to have Cole back.

"I really enjoyed preaching on Sundays for the first few weeks, but boy, am I glad you're back," she said. "Preparing a sermon every week sort of reminded me of taking exams in college."

The church construction projects were either finished or soon would be. The congregation was growing. Even though the sanctuary had been enlarged, it was full on Sunday mornings. Perhaps the church needed to have two worship services each week, but for the moment, Cole liked to see the sanctuary full on Sundays.

One morning, as Cole drove into work, he saw a man on the roadside with a sign that read, "Have hungry family—Will work for food." Stopping his car, Cole waited for the man to walk up to him.

"Tell me about your hungry family," Cole said. "I'm a preacher, and perhaps I can help."

"Parson, thanks for stopping," the man replied. "Haven't had much luck this morning. I have a wife and three little ones out at the camp. We moved here from Mississippi looking for work, but there's not much out here."

"What camp are you talking about?" Cole asked.

"Why, you being a preacher, I figured you had seen it."

"Can't say that I have, but I might like to. How many people live there?" Cole asked.

"Seems like there's about twenty-five or thirty families now, but they say the number goes down in the cold months," the man replied.

"Tell me your name, and I will see what we can do about some food."

"Name's Judd French. 'Preciate your help, but I'm scared of that big animal in your back seat."

"He won't bite," Cole said. "Hop in the car with me, and we'll see about finding some food."

Stopping at Sunshine Grocery, Cole introduced French to the owner, a member of Cole's church, and said, "Mr. French, get a cart and fill it up, and I will pay for it."

After his cart was full, Cole paid for the groceries and followed the directions to a wooded area about a mile out of town. People and tents were scattered throughout the woods.

"What can I do to pay for these groceries?" French asked.

"Do you have a car or truck?" Cole asked.

"Yes, we have an old truck."

"Tomorrow, I would like for you to come to the church at ten and talk to some folks about food and hunger; we can tell them about a crazy idea I have."

The next morning, at Cole's request, all six members of the church finance committee gathered in Cole's office. As usual, Cole had coffee and doughnuts waiting for them.

Martha Franks was quick to say, "Cole, is this another one of your surprises? You're not going somewhere, are you?"

"No, Martha, nothing like that, but I do want to describe an experience I had yesterday morning just outside of town. I saw a man standing on the side of the road with a sign that said, 'I will work for food.' Now I would like for you to meet Judd French and let him tell you his story."

And French did, describing his search for work and his struggle to feed his family. Only two committee members were aware of the encampment, and none had seen it. After they discussed it, Cole said, "I've got some ideas about how we might help. As I'm sure you know, there is a large field near the educational building.

"When I was a boy in Memphis, my father agreed to let me play baseball and miss church on Sundays if I would help a family by raising a garden, which I did for three months in the summer. My idea is to plow the field up and let it sit until spring. Denmark does not have a farmer's market. We could easily raise enough money to feed the families, especially those with small children. In addition, it would provide jobs for those who would like to work in the garden. The Bible is clear about feeding the less fortunate. Money from the sale of fruits and vegetables should be enough to provide food for all the families in the winter months. What do you think?"

"Who owns that field?" Roger Simpson asked. "I would think it might be expensive."

Cole smiled. "I do. I bought it back when I bought my house. At the time, I didn't know what I might do with it, but I figured it being close to the church would come in handy at some point. This is some point. My plan is to lease it to the church for a dollar a year."

Another member asked, "What do you think of the idea, Mr. French?"

"Just glad I was standing on the side of the road when the preacher came along!" he replied. "It would give me a way to feed my family."

Martha Franks held up her hand just as the meeting was about to end. "Cole, I hate to ask you this, but who is going to be in charge if you're not here? What are your plans? Is it baseball or church?"

"Martha, that's a good question," Cole responded. "Right now, the Yankees have not been in contact with me. Tracey and I have not discussed it. However, if I ever did return to New York, I can assure you this church and this garden project would be taken care of."

The next afternoon, just after lunch, Josh Palmer came calling.

"Cole, nice to see you again," he said, settling into a chair in Cole's office. They chatted a bit before getting down to business. "Hope you had time to rest and think about next season. You remember what the offer is, a million dollars up front as a signing bonus and double your last salary."

"To be honest, Josh, I really haven't thought about it," Cole replied. "Been too busy catching up with the church and my family. I'm not at all sure what I'm going to do. Give me ten days to make my decision."

That night, after supper was done and the baby was in bed, Cole and Tracey cuddled up on the couch to talk.

"The first thing I want to tell you is how the meeting went in the church. None of them were aware that over a hundred people live just outside of Denmark on land owned by the county. It used to be an airfield. Some live in old campers, but most live in tents. I saw several children there—who knows where their food comes from?" Cole said. "The committee members were surprised when they found out I had purchased the land next to the educational building."

The garden would have to wait until spring, he said, though they could cut the grass and put a sign up about the garden ministry.

"That really sounds great, and there were no other questions?" Tracey asked.

"Well, there is one other topic we need to talk about. Martha Franks asked me how we could do a ministry like this if I was in New York playing baseball. And I might have an answer for that. What would you think if I only played baseball for part of the season?"

"Would the Yankees agree to that?"

"That's an interesting point," Cole responded. "But there's only one way to find out."

Tracey hesitated. He could tell she had something to say but was reluctant to say it.

"What are you thinking?" he pressed.

"I planned to wait to tell you this, but now seems to be the best time. I've been feeling a little funny the last few weeks. I knew what the problem was but decided to have the doctor look me over. Turned out I was right. Cole, you better sit down before I tell you this."

"You're not . . . you don't have—" Cole stuttered, with memories of losing Diane to cancer years ago.

"No, no, nothing bad," she rushed to reassure him, "but we may have to add another bedroom."

"You're going to have a baby?"

Tracey kissed his cheek and whispered into his ear: "Get ready. Not one but two. Looks like Luke is going to have lots of company."

Cole was stupefied, then thrilled, and hugged his wife gently. "Oh, my!" he grinned.

Ten days later, Josh Palmer was back in Cole's office with a contract to be signed. "Cole, you ready to sign up for another season?"

"No, Josh, I cannot be away from the church and my family for that long."

Seeing the disappointment on Palmer's face, Cole pitched his counterproposal.

"What if I agree to a shorter season, starting in June? That way I would be with you through the heart of season and the playoffs, and the World Series if we make it that far."

"I don't much think New York would go for it. Never done anything like that."

"Well, give it a try. I'd like to play baseball for another year. Pretty sure the Red Sox would take me if the Yankees don't."

Not pleased with that, Palmer said, "I'll be back in a week or so."

With time to spare, Cole called Britches to tell him about the conversation with Palmer. Britches answered, as cheery as ever. "Hey, Cole, what's up? In just three weeks, I'll be your brother-in-law."

After a few minutes, Cole revealed his reply to the Yankees' offer.

"Bet you five to one they say yes," Britches said, chuckling. "They would be foolish not to. And I'm sure they did not like you mentioning the Red Sox."

As Britches predicted, Palmer was back a week later with a new contract. Cole would don a Yankees uniform in June.

The following Sunday, Cole told the church members about his decision to play baseball for three months with the Yankees. Following that, he told them about the plan to provide food as needed for the families in the tent city.

Later that afternoon, Cole called Luther to catch up. Before Cole could say anything, Luther said, "We was getting ready to call you. Big news—Socrates is leaving the Cardinals. He's got a job teaching history at his old high school, and he's going to coach baseball. Pearly and me, we're pretty excited. Now what's your news?"

Not ready to mention Tracey being pregnant, Cole told Luther about his contract with New York and about the garden.

"Good news 'bout the contract with New York," Luther said. "Be better for your arm. You're no spring chicken anymore. Now tell me—how big is that garden?"

"About ten times the size of the one Nancy Wilson had."

"Oh, my, pretty big. I'll take a look at it when we come to Denmark to get Britches married."

To build awareness, Cole had the grass cut and a sign made that read, "Presbyterian Garden Ministry." Next, he had small signs made with the names of the fruits and vegetables they planned to plant. Now they just had to wait for spring.

A month later, guests arrived to celebrate the marriage of Britches and Sandra. Luther and Pearly were first to arrive, followed by Nancy Wilson and her new husband.

A day after his arrival, Luther toured the new garden site with Cole.

"My, my," Luther said. "This is big enough to feed most of Denmark as well as them homeless people. I'll be back in the spring to help you lay it out."

Two days before the wedding, Britches stopped by the church with a worried look on his face. "Hey, Cole, you remember I was your best man when you got married."

"Seems like I remember that," Cole said.

"And if you're my best man, who is gonna marry us? You can't be both preacher and best man."

"Well then, I suppose we'll just have to postpone the wedding until late summer when one of my brothers could be here."

"No, no, that would be terrible. We want to get married."

"Let's get Pepper in here and see what she has to say."

When Pepper heard the problem, she laughed and said, "Not sure I could help; I've never been a best man before."

"Not funny," Britches said. "You two are fooling me."

"Britches, you are so excited that you forgot my brother Bill is coming from Atlanta to perform the ceremony," Cole said. "After the joke you pulled on me when I got married, I should have let you worry."

Two days later, Sandra and Steve Malone (also known as "Britches") were married. The church was full to overflowing, as was the country club.

A handful of Yankees teammates and a few from the Tigers had come to Denmark for the wedding. Many of them had been victims of Britches's practical jokes, and they intended to return the favor. At the reception, just before the wedding cake was cut, one of them pretended to drop something on the floor. While bending over to pick it up, he slipped a set of handcuffs on Britches's ankle and attached the other cuff to a table. With yells and laughter, they said, "Don't you worry, Britches, we'll take care of your bride for you!"

After much pleading from the bride, Britches was released, the cake was cut, and the bride and groom escaped to Bermuda.

Tracey waited until a few days after the wedding to tell everyone the news they were expecting twins in the spring. Cole told Luther and Pearly about it before they left for Memphis. Luther said, "Take care of your arm—you may have to pitch for ten years to pay for this!"

Cole also told his brother before he left for Atlanta and then called his parents in Memphis. On Sunday after church, Tracey told the church members about the babies, and the news was out!

Garden
Ministry

In mid-February, there was a break in the weather, and Luther drove back to Denmark to lay out the garden. "This looks to me to be seven or eight times larger than the one we planted for Mrs. Wilson. After we get it plowed up real good, we can lay it out. Going to take a lot of hoeing and chopping to keep the grass from coming back. Be worth it, though, to make sure you have plenty of turnip greens!"

By mid-March, the ground was ready for planting. Judd French brought six men from the encampment, and four church officers joined them. Ten days later, all the vegetables were in the ground, and more than two hundred tomato plants were planted and staked.

When the vegetables were ready to be picked, the garden ministry proved to be a success. Every day, the church delivered food to the camp. When people from other churches realized that all the garden money was being used to support the camp, they volunteered to work along with the Presbyterians.

One evening, Cole was telling Tracey about how well the garden was doing. "We have enough money to get us through the winter and into the next spring," he said. As he continued talking about the garden plans, Tracey interrupted.

"Wait, wait, stop. It's time to go."

Cole, not realizing what she was talking about, continued to tell her about the garden.

"Where are the car keys right now, Cole? It's time to quit talking about raising a garden and start talking about raising some children! Where are the keys?"

"Oh—oh!" Cole suddenly realized what was happening and began searching for the keys. "They're in my pants pocket, but where are my pants?"

"You have them on, Cole. Look in your back pocket. Are you okay to drive? You look pretty rattled."

"Yes, I'm fine, just a little excited." Fifteen minutes later, they arrived at the hospital, and six hours after that, two little girls named Catherine and Anna Marie joined the family.

Four days later, Tracey and the babies were home from the hospital. Sandra came to help with the two newborns, and one-year-old Luther Cole tried to help but soon became adept at staying out of the way.

In only ten days, Cole would depart for New York. Last year's failed season was still on his mind. How had that happened? Most people felt the Yankees had the best players. The Yankees had a long tradition of being World Series champions. However, it had not happened that way. It would be different this time.

Since the beginning of the season, Britches had called to report on the team and the new lineup. After last year, a personnel shakeup was expected and delivered. Offseason departures cut the payroll and allowed the Yankees to rebuild. On paper, they were much stronger than the previous year. And yet the team struggled early on.

Cole's thoughts turned back to Denmark. The church was doing well and continuing to grow. The construction projects were on schedule or nearly finished. Soon the church might have to consider adding another service, but that project could wait a little while.

Every day, the church garden sold out of vegetables, and workers from the garden made trips to nearby orchards to buy peaches and apples for resale. As Cole's departure grew near, Pepper took over managing the church's project.

Cole left for New York in June. It was hard to leave behind Tracey and the babies, hard to leave the church and its projects, and hard to leave Denmark.

How easy it would be to call Tracey and tell her the team suddenly woke up and began winning games as soon as he returned to New York. It didn't happen that way. In fact, the Yankees got worse.

After losing the first of a series against the Braves, moods in the clubhouse were grim.

Before the second game began, a manager gave a speech meant to motivate the team before he and the coaches stepped out to confer. The players were alone for a few minutes. Cole stood and cleared his throat. Before he could begin, Simmons, the team's shortstop, said, "What's up, Cole? You gonna preach to us? Because if you are, I don't intend to listen."

"You shut up, Simmons, or I'll make you shut up," Cole quickly responded.

"I didn't return to the Yankees for money. I don't play for the money, and most of you don't, either. I did not come back to pitch for a team in last place. I did not come back to play for a team in second place. I came back for only one reason. We failed last season. I do not intend for that to happen again. We are known as 'the world champion New York Yankees.' Let's prove it! Let's prove it today and every day we have left to play."

For whatever reason, the Yankees seemed to wake up. They beat the Braves in the next two games and were about to turn a corner, finally. They came back from the All-Star break fresh and ready, winning eight consecutive games.

By August, they were unbeatable and soon swept the Red Sox aside on the way to the playoffs.

To no one's surprise, the Yankees quickly swept through the playoffs and headed to the World Series once again. They would play last year's winners, the Philadelphia Phillies.

The first two games took place in New York. Cole's dad, his brothers, Luther, and Pearly sat right behind the New York dugout. Once again, his mom had gone to Denmark to help Tracey, and he knew they were watching with the rest of the town.

As Game One began, the Phillies players were quick to begin yelling insults at the Yankees players, especially Cole. "Hey, Preacher, nice to see you—thought you were in a nursing home."

"Don't listen," Britches muttered. "We'll shut them up."

Britches, who was having the best year of his career, hit a home run in the last inning. It didn't help much, however. The final score was Phillies 6, New York 1. The Yankees had been humiliated but rebounded to win Game Two, 3–1.

They went to Philadelphia for the next three games, and the Series went back and forth with no clear winner in sight. The Yankees won Games Three and Four; the Phillies took Game Five. Game Six was in New York. If the Yankees took this game, they would win it all!

Just before the start of the game, Britches came to check on Cole.

"You all right?" Britches asked.

"No, not at all," Cole replied. "Been throwing up for over an hour. I can't seem to keep anything down, and now I'm freezing."

The team doctor was sitting with Cole. Looking toward Britches, he said, "It's not good. He can't keep anything down. Temperature is pretty close to 102. He can't play."

"The hell I can't," Cole insisted. "I waited all my life for this."

By then, the pitching coach and the manager had joined the group.

"Let's just see what happens," the manager said. "Maybe Crenshaw can hold them. He's got the same damn bug, but he's had plenty of rest. Let's just keep our fingers crossed."

As soon as Crenshaw started pitching, it was obvious he was not right. He was as sick as Cole. With three runs, a man on first base, and no outs, the pitching coach told the doctor to get Cole ready.

"Okay," the doctor said. "Get Cole to drink this and give him another anti-nausea pill, and let's see. Only thing I know to do. Britches, you go in with him, and prayer is our best chance."

"Get me three innings if you possibly can," the pitching coach said to Cole.

"Give me the ball and a little room," Cole said. "I'm going to have to throw up again."

"Just think of Tracey and Luke and the twins; you'll be home soon," Britches said.

When Cole walked toward the pitcher's mound, some of the Phillies players began yelling. News that Cole and some of the other Yankees had a stomach bug gave them plenty of ammunition.

"Hey, Adams! You want a doctor?"

"Don't throw up, Cole! You're on national television! You got 50,000 people here in the ballpark who don't want to see you puke!"

There's only one way to shut them up, Cole thought, and he took his place on the pitcher's mound.

The first batter grounded out, and the next two struck out. Some of the noise from the Phillies dugout died down. Between innings, coaches kept cool towels on Cole and gave him sports drinks to keep him hydrated.

The third inning was a turning point. With two runners on base, Britches hit a line drive off the left-field wall. Both runners scored. At the end of the third inning, the Yankees were ahead, 4–3. As the game went on, Cole seemed to grow weaker, but somehow, as he mixed pitches, speeds, and locations, the Phillies still did not get a hit.

In the fifth, the Yankees' bats were on fire, and the score was 7–3 by the end of the inning. There still was a lot of game left to play, however, and Cole felt his own downward trajectory.

Heading for the dugout, Cole stumbled. Britches caught him and walked with him.

If New York could somehow hold on, they would be the World Series champions. How to get that done was another matter.

With the Phillies watching the Yankees' dugout to see who the next pitcher might be, Cole slowly walked toward the mound with Britches and the four Yankees infielders walking with him. As they did so, Cole's cheering section lit up. His first pitch hit the batter. Cole walked the second batter on four pitches, none of which were close to the plate.

The Yankees manager called timeout, and the pitching coach walked to the mound. "Skipper says we want to go with you. Got no one else who can step in. Crenshaw's a mess. You're the best we got. Win or lose, it's your game."

The next batter fouled off two pitches before striking out, and the following batter hit a sharp groundball to the shortstop for an easy double play to end the inning. Once again, the Yankees' bats were silent, and they went quietly into the eighth.

Britches and the entire Yankees infield walked with Cole to the mound again.

With his back to the infield, Cole whispered, "Britches, do you remember the grip on the softball Pepper used to put a reverse spin on the ball? I'm going to try it. You watch out because the ball is going to break in to right-handed batters and away from left-handed batters."

The result was unhittable. The first batter watched them call the third strike. The second batter managed two foul balls before striking out, and the third batter did no better. Cole struck out the side; only one more inning to go, and the Yankees would win the World Series. In the dugout, the team doctor gave him a hot liquid that tasted like turpentine.

New York had done nothing when they batted in the seventh and eighth, so it all came down to the final Phillies batters. Cole was exhausted. All the fans jumped to their feet, cheering for either Atlanta or New York. Players in both dugouts were standing.

"I don't see how he could possibly pitch one more inning," the pitching coach whispered. "Never seen anything like this before. A little bit of arm and an awful lot of heart."

Cole stepped out of the dugout. Above the roar of the crowd, Cole could hear Luther and his dad yelling, "Just a few more, Cole! You can do it!"

As Cole went to the mound, the entire team surrounded him.

"Here we go," Britches said. "Can you do it?"

"Just give me the ball. Only one way to find out."

The next batter was a first baseman who had already hit a couple of home runs and had four other hits in the first five games—although he had no hits against Cole. Trying to keep the batter off balance, Cole kept the balls inside with late-breaking pitches. The batter did not swing, even though the count was two strikes and no balls. Cole changed his grip on the ball, moving his finger back, a trick he had learned from Pepper and her softball. The next pitch was waist high and over the middle of the plate. As the batter swung, the ball dropped sharply and away from him. Strike three. The second batter struck out on three pitches. Only one Phillies batter was left, and the Yankees were about to win it all.

As the last batter came to the plate, Cole again felt a chill surging over him. For a moment, he was dizzy with severe stomach cramps. Calling timeout, the pitching coach and Britches gathered around him. "Do you want to come out, Cole? There's only one more batter, and it's over."

"No! No, no, no. This game is mine. Just give me the ball and let me finish it. And Britches, all curves. I want to finish with a strikeout before I throw up again."

All the fans were on their feet, yelling and cheering. The Yankees players were standing in front of the dugout, hoping the game was about to end.

"You okay?" Britches asked.

"I feel bad, but my arm is fine. Get ready. The last Phillies hitter is a left-handed eddying center fielder."

Once again, with Cole using Pepper's softball grips, the first pitch sailed over the middle of the plate. The pitch dropped, and the batter swung and missed. The second pitch was more of the same, and once again the batter swung and missed. As the entire stadium of fans stood up, Cole delivered a fastball in the middle of the plate. As the batter swung, the pitch seemed to collapse, and the batter missed again.

The game was over. The Yankees had won. They were World Series champions. Cole had struck out seventeen of the twenty-seven batters he had faced. He had pitched nine innings in relief and had not allowed a hit. As the Yankees players carried Cole off the field, the Phillies players stood outside their dugout with their hats off as a sign of respect.

As Cole neared the dugout, he could hear people yelling to him. His parents were there, though he didn't see them. Even above the noise of the crowd, he could hear Luther saying, "Never seen anything like that!"

Morgan, the second baseman, put his arm around Cole's shoulders. "Well done, Cole. I didn't know that you were going to strike them all out. I could have stayed in the dugout. You're something else."

Despite the celebration and excitement, Cole continued to have stomach cramps, chills, and fever. Slipping away, he called a cab, took the medicines the team doctor had given him, and went to bed.

Two days later, the entire city turned out for a ticker-tape parade. On the day after the parade, Cole was preparing to catch a plane to Atlanta when he heard a knock on his door. Expecting Britches, he was surprised to find Josh Palmer.

"Didn't want to let you get away before I talked to you," Palmer said. "You made baseball history with your performance in the World Series. You will receive a substantial bonus for the team winning the American League pennant and another for defeating Philadelphia in the World Series. You may not remember the terms of your contract, but a bonus clause for individual performance came into play. The total of these is well above a million dollars, which you will receive next week.

"Now, here's the thing I would like for you to consider. I know it's hard for you to think about this, but if you choose to come back and sign a new contract, you will receive over a million-dollar signing bonus, and your salary next year will be more than double what it was this year. For now, go home and celebrate. I will touch base with you after Thanksgiving."

"I really can't think about that right now," Cole replied. "Let's just leave it open. I have my wife, my little boy, and my twin girls waiting on me and a church to look after."

In Atlanta, a limo and driver were waiting on Cole and Britches. The same driver who had carried Cole to the tryouts two years ago said, "I feel pretty honored to be taking you gentlemen for a ride, famous as you are."

"I feel pretty honored for you to be taking us home," Britches responded.

As they approached Denmark, they could see a large crowd waiting on the church steps with ribbons, flags, and a banner that said, "Welcome Home, World Series Champions!" Tracey, holding Catherine, stood with Luke and Sandra, who was holding Anna Marie, on the church steps. Luke toddled over to jump into his dad's arms, and Cole reached out his hand to Tracey. Sandra walked to stand beside Britches, who hugged her gently.

The mayor of Denmark presented keys to the city to both of them.

"Cole and Britches, we are so proud of both of you," he said. "We are going to have a citywide barbecue for you in your honor. This year, we have a special presentation from the pitcher on the Denmark Baptist baseball team."

Stepping up to the podium, the Denmark Baptist pitcher said, "Cole, a couple years ago, you hit a home run and the Presbyterians were city champions. Our team has talked it over, and we decided that if the Philadelphia Phillies professional baseball team can't hit your pitching, then the Denmark Baptists can't, either. So here is the trophy the Presbyterians won last year. In your honor, we give it back to you to keep for another year."

Cole set Luke down, and took the trophy to hold it aloft.

"This trophy is for all of us," he said. "I was fortunate to be called here to be a preacher, then to leave you for a short time to play baseball. Now I'm blessed to come home and be part of Denmark again. And how lucky I was to have Britches Malone, another Denmark resident, as my catcher and teammate. He's not only my Yankees teammate, but he has been my best friend for more than twenty years."

At his feet, Luke began pulling at his dad's pocket and whimpering.

"My son has had about all the baseball he can stand, and he is telling me, 'Let's go home,'" Cole laughed. "I wish I had a World Series trophy to show you, but that stays in New York. For now, the church league trophy will be enough. Britches and I thank you for this celebration. Come to church on Sunday."

On Sunday morning, as Cole closed his sermon, he reflected, "We began our service with that wonderful hymn, written so long ago. 'Great is Thy faithfulness; morning by morning, new mercies I see.' And I close today with a portion of Psalm 98, 'Shout joyfully to the Lord, all the earth, break forth in song, rejoice and sing praises.' Look around you; we are growing. Our congregation is growing. Our young people are growing. Even our building is growing. How blessed we are! Amen."

It was a storybook ending, the way it was supposed to happen. A few days earlier, Britches and Cole had sat on the backs of convertibles for a ticker-tape parade through downtown New York, and then they returned home to a joyous welcome in Denmark. Now, at last, they were home for good.

For the next week, Cole stayed at home playing with the three babies. Late one afternoon, a week later, Tracey came home to find the babysitter taking care of the children.

Looking for Cole, she heard a loud thump outside near the barn and went to investigate.

Just as she expected, she found Cole throwing baseballs.

www.ingramcontent.com/pod-product-compliance
Lightning Source LLC
Chambersburg PA
CBHW060624310726
48982CB00003B/671